The Screech Owls' Home Loss

Roy MacGregor

An M&S Paperback Original from
McClelland & Stewart Inc.
The Canadian Publishers

For Miss Mern Parker, grades 3–5, Huntsville Public School 1955–57. "A teacher's teacher."

The author is grateful to Doug Gibson, who thought up this series, and to Alex Schultz, who pulls it off.

An M&S Paperback Original from
McClelland & Stewart Inc.

Canadian Cataloguing in Publication Data

MacGregor, Roy, 1948–
   The Screech Owls' home loss

(The Screech Owls series)
"An M&S paperback original".
ISBN 0-7710-5618-4

I. Title.   II. Series: MacGregor, Roy, 1948–   .
The Screech Owls series.

PS8575.G84S37 1998   jC813'.54   C98-930901-0
PZ7.M32SC 1998

We acknowledge the financial support of the Government of Canada through the Book Publishing Industry Development Program for our publishing activities.

Cover illustration by Gregory C. Banning
Typeset in Bembo by M&S, Toronto

Printed and bound in Canada

McClelland & Stewart Inc.
The Canadian Publishers
481 University Avenue
Toronto, Ontario
M5G 2E9

   1 2 3 4 5   02 01 00 99 98

"*LOOK OUTSIDE!*"

It seemed such an absurd order; Travis Lindsay could not yet see *inside*, let alone look out. His eyes were still sticky with sleep, his mind in another world. His own voice seemed like it belonged to some dim-witted creature, not even human, as he tried to speak into the cordless phone.

"*Whuh?*"

"*Look outside!*" Nish shouted again at the other end, loud enough this time that Travis's mother, still standing by the bed after handing her son the telephone, heard and answered for him.

"*He's awake, Nish!*" she called out towards the receiver. Travis blinked upwards. His mother was laughing at him as he struggled to surface from a deep, deep sleep.

"Nish is right," Mrs. Lindsay said to Travis. "Get up and have a look."

Travis rubbed his eyes. He checked the clock radio: 7:03 a.m. Too early even for school. And it was *Saturday*, wasn't it? *What was Nish up to?*

"*He's moving, Nish!*" Mrs. Lindsay called towards the receiver.

Travis set the phone down on his pillow and pushed back his covers. He instantly wished he could dive straight back under them, burrowing into their warmth and slipping back into the magnificent sleep that had just been stolen from him. He fought off the urge and struggled to his feet, stretching and yawning hard as his mother, still laughing, stepped back to let him pass. Behind her, Travis could see his father standing in the doorway with a cup of coffee in his hand. He was trying to blow onto the steaming cup, but he couldn't purse his lips properly. He was laughing too. *What on earth could be so funny about looking outside?*

Travis scratched his side and chewed on the stale taste of sleep as he all but staggered towards the window. His mother reached out in front of him, yanking the heavy curtains back.

Travis reacted as if he'd just been blindsided by a hard check. The window seemed to explode with light, like a million flashbulbs firing at once.

He stepped back, his hands over his eyes. In the background he could hear Nish's voice squeaking like a mouse as he continued to shout over the telephone, which lay, completely ignored, on Travis's pillow.

Travis rubbed his eyes hard, the light still flashing red and yellow and orange in the front of his brain. He rubbed and waited, peeking first through his fingers as he approached the window again. It was still too bright, the light like blinding needles, but slowly his eyes adjusted. Still squinting, he moved closer to the window, the glass quickly fogging with his breath, then clearing as he stood back slightly.

The world had turned to glass!

Travis looked out over the backyard, out past Sarah Cuthbertson's big house on the hill, and off towards the river and the lookout that sat high over the town of Tamarack. *Glass!* Glass everywhere: shining, sparkling, silver down along the river, golden along the tip of Lookout Hill where the sun was just cresting, hard steel along the streets of the town that lay still shaded for the moment by the hills to the east.

The window was fogging up again. Travis pressed a fist against the cold glass, circling to clear the window. The condensation clung to his skin, cold and wet and tickling.

He blinked again. The sight reminded Travis of a counter at the jewellery store owned by Fahd's uncle, diamonds shimmering under bright lights, expensive crystal glittering on glass displays.

A town truck was moving down River Street, heading for the road up towards the lookout. The truck was spreading a shower of sand, the silver road turning brown as the truck crept slowly along. But at the turn for the bridge and the hill, the truck kept sliding down River Street, the wheels spinning uselessly, the big vehicle turning, slowly, like a large boat, until eventually it crunched sideways into an ice-covered snowbank.

Travis could see children outside a home on King Street. They were stepping as if they were walking on a tightrope rather than a wide street. One went down, smack on his back, and slid helplessly. The other youngster leapt after the first one, spinning wildly.

There was an urgent squeak at Travis's ear.

"*Ya see it?*"

Travis turned quickly, almost jumping. His mother was holding the phone out for him. He had forgotten all about Nish!

Travis took the phone. "*Neat!*"

"*Whatdya mean, 'neat'?*" Nish's voice now barked clearly over the telephone. "*It's awesome! It's amazing! It's unbelievable! C'mon — we gotta get out on it. Grab your skates!*"

Nish didn't even wait for an answer. He slammed his own phone down so hard Travis winced.

Grab your skates? It looked more like Travis should be grabbing a rope and a bucket of sand — perhaps even his father's spike-soled golf shoes — to walk on that. But he saw Nish's point: Tamarack had turned into the world's largest skating rink.

"It's called *verglas*," said Mr. Lindsay after Travis had handed his mother back the cordless phone. "At least that's what my friend Doug's grandfather called it. He was an old Scot, and he said he'd seen it only three times in his life. This is the second time for me."

"What is it?" Travis asked. He was back at the window, clearing a porthole with the side of his fist.

"You have to have a deep thaw followed immediately by a deep freeze – and no snow in between. It's a freak of nature. Beautiful – but dangerous."

Travis looked out and thought about the last week. Tamarack had seen record snowfalls through January – the snow was piled so high along the streets that pedestrians stumbling along the sidewalks couldn't see the cars passing alongside them. But then, on the first of February, a south wind came in, bringing record-high temperatures. Nish had even turned up for hockey practice in shorts and sunglasses.

Then it had rained. Not enough to melt the snow, but enough to turn the streets to ponds. And just last night the winds had suddenly shifted, and a bitter cold front had moved in from the north. The thermometer outside the kitchen window had fallen so fast it seemed to have sprung a leak. The cold was so deep that twice during the evening the Lindsays had gone to the window when maple trees in the backyard had cracked like rifle fire.

"That's what Old Man Gibson called it," said Mr. Lindsay. "*Verglas*. It don't know what it means.

Gaelic for something to do with 'glass,' I suppose. You can see why."

"How long did it last?" asked Mrs. Lindsay.

"Only a couple of days. But if I had to pick two winter days out of my childhood I'd never want to forget, I'd probably take those two. Maybe because they closed the schools down and no one could even get to work."

"They closed the schools?" asked Travis.

"It's Saturday," said Travis's mother, crushing his hopes.

Mr. Lindsay went on, lost in his own memories: "They put chains over their car tires back then. That was before they sanded the roads. The chains would bite into the ice so they could get a grip. We used to grab onto the back bumpers of the cars and they'd drag us on our rubber boots up and down the streets."

"*Charles!*" Mrs. Lindsay said abruptly.

But Mr. Lindsay was laughing, enjoying a sweet memory. "We called it 'hitching.' It was kind of like waterskiing, except it was winter, and we were being pulled around by cars, not motorboats."

"You're lucky you weren't killed," said Mrs. Lindsay.

"I guess," Mr. Lindsay answered slowly. "But cars went a lot slower back then, and there weren't as many on the road."

"*Still!*" she said.

"You're right. I wouldn't recommend it now. But you kids should get out there and skate on it. It's a once-in-a-lifetime experience."

"You've seen it twice," Travis corrected.

"Yes," his father said. "But I was only young once."

Mr. Lindsay went to the window. He was smiling, but it seemed to Travis a sad smile. Then his father turned, slapping his hands together to break the spell.

"You'd better get dressed, young man."

Travis looked out in the direction his father had been gazing. A thick-set young man in a blue Screech Owls jacket and cap was churning full force around the corner, his skates digging deep where normally there would have been pavement.

The young skater kicked out suddenly and flew through the air – like a wrestler going for the throat – until he slammed, side down and laughing, onto the slope of the road. The ice offered no resistance, and followed by his stick, gloves, and hat, the youngster came spinning and sliding like a fat hockey puck straight towards the Lindsay driveway.

It was Nish, coming to call.

2

ONE BY ONE, THE SCREECH OWLS FOUND EACH other. It was as if centre ice had become the intersection of River and Cedar and Muck had blown his whistle for them all to assemble. Sarah was out – her long, graceful stride as powerful and elegant down River Street as it had ever been at the Tamarack Memorial Arena. Lars Johanssen, with two sticks over his shoulder, came kicking a puck between his skates along Cedar Street. Jeremy Weathers, stiff and unsure in his goalie skates, came with Dmitri Yakushev from the apartments down by the frozen river. Data, Fahd Noorizadeh, Gordie Griffith, Jesse Highboy, Andy Higgins, little Simon Milliken, Liz Moscovitz, Chantal Larochelle, Jenny Staples in her goalie skates and thick street-hockey pads, carrying a bent and torn street-hockey net over her shoulder. From the other direction, pushing an equally bent and torn net ahead of him as he skated towards the gathering of Owls, came Derek Dillinger.

"*Not here!*" shouted Nish, whose face was already beet red and covered in sweat.

"Where, then?" Jenny shouted, dropping the net with a clatter.

"*The creek!*"

Of course, the creek. Behind Derek Dillinger's house was a large field belonging to Derek's uncle, who grew corn and oats and raised beef on the edge of town. A creek ran from the woods and twisted down through the fields, past the school and the rink, and emptied into the river.

A few times in other winters they had gone out with shovels and cleared off an area for a game of shinny. It was hard work, though, and the ice was often bumpy, with cracks that could catch a skate blade and twist an ankle. Today's ice, however, was as smooth as marble.

"*Let's go!*" Derek shouted.

They skated down the streets and across the lawns. They dug in to go up hills and leaned back to go down them. They skated to the end of King Street, crossed the glassed-over highway, then slid down the embankment and under the barbed-wire fence – now rendered harmless by thick sleeves of crystal-clear ice – to where the frozen creek spread across the open field.

Nish had chosen well. At first they were content just to skate around the field, laughing as they danced through the corn stubble on the far side, and then barrelling together through a stand of bulrushes that snapped and shattered like fine glass as they passed, the sparkling shards ringing on the ice as they spun away.

"*Let's play!*" Travis shouted. He was captain. He was taking charge.

Travis threw his stick down, and the others followed suit. Travis then waded into the pile, randomly grabbing up and tossing the sticks, half of them towards Nish, half towards Data.

"You two are the captains," he said.

Travis finished dividing the sticks and stood back. "Pick up your sticks and stay with your captain," he said. The Owls chased after their sticks, picked them up, and began looking around to see who was playing with whom. Sarah reached out and gently slapped Dmitri's tuque; the two linemates were still together.

"No fair!" said Nish. "They got all the speed."

"Don't worry about it," Travis said. "We'll make them play into the wind."

"Yeah," Nish said, looking up with a sly grin. "Good idea."

Travis told Jeremy to take one of the nets and start skating until he reached the gate at the far end of the field. Jenny was to take her net and head towards the fence by the road. The distance between the nets would be, approximately, four hockey rinks. The fences on either side of the field would form the "boards."

"What're the rules?" asked Fahd, who always had to know the rules.

"There are none," said Nish, with a fake snarl.

"No body contact," said Travis. "No hoists on goal. No slapshots. Everything else goes."

And everything did. With no offsides, Nish, with his good wristshot, could make a pass that almost took the puck out of sight before Travis, bolting across the field at top speed, caught up with it and came down, coasting, onto the flat ice of the creek and in on Jenny, who was backing up fast and kicking out her foam-rubber pads in anticipation.

Travis came in and stopped hard, the good sharp of his skates sending up a swirl of snow that temporarily blinded them both as it flashed like fireworks in the sun. Jenny instinctively turned from the spray, and Travis, laughing, tucked the puck behind her on an easy backhand.

"*Cheater!*" Jenny shouted. But she, too, was laughing.

Sarah and Dmitri got the goal back quickly on a European-style, circling, end-to-end "rush" that took almost five minutes and left the two of them, and every other Screech Owl, flat on their backs and gasping for air.

"In Russia," Dmitri said, panting, "we call this *bandy*."

"In Canada," growled Nish, also short of breath and flat on his back, "we call it 'hog.'"

"No," said Dmitri, "really – *bandy* is a game. Curved sticks, a ball, a huge ice surface like this, and lots and lots of players. Hockey developed from it."

"Russia *invented* hockey?" said Nish with enormous suspicion. "Is that what you're saying?"

"As much as anyone else did, I guess."

Nish howled with laughter. "And what else did you invent? Big Macs? Nintendo? *The wheel?*"

"Who do *you* think invented it?"

"We did, of course. The Stanley Cup is *Canadian*, not *Russian* – or perhaps you didn't notice."

"There are paintings," countered Dmitri, "that show kids playing something that looks a lot like hockey in Holland more than five hundred years ago."

"Paintings aren't photographs," said Nish.

"*What?*" said Sarah, sitting up, a look of astonishment on her face.

"You can paint anything you want. I want proof."

"They didn't *have* cameras five hundred years ago!" Sarah shouted.

"That's just my point," he said, smiling smugly. "Then there's no real proof, is there."

"You're impossible!" said Sarah, scrambling to her feet.

"You're nuts!" said Dmitri, also getting up.

"I'm right," said Nish. "And you all know it."

Travis lay on the ice, shaking his head in amazement at the ridiculous way Nish's brain could sometimes work. He'd seen it in school a few times, and he'd seen teachers stare at Nish as if he'd just been dropped in on the classroom from another planet.

"*Will you look at that!*" Sarah shouted as she bent to pick up her stick.

Everyone turned to see. At the far end of the field, four large figures were standing at the fence, trying to figure out how to get over. Then one climbed up, leapt over the top, and landed on his skates, sliding and shouting. It was Ty, the Owls' assistant coach. And right behind Ty, also leaping over the iced-over barbed wire, was Barry, the other assistant, also in skates. And behind Barry, tossing over a pile of hockey sticks, was Mr. Dillinger, his bald head covered only with earmuffs, which seemed hopelessly inadequate.

And right behind Mr. Dillinger was *Muck!*

Mr. Dillinger's brother, the farmer who owned these fields, must have telephoned him, and Mr. Dillinger – who could never turn down a chance to be a kid again – must have called the two assistant coaches, who also loved to play shinny.

But Muck?

Muck Munro wasn't one for playing around. The coach often suggested to the Owls that a game of street hockey or a round of pond shinny was twice as good as a practice, but for him to come out and play as well was very, very unusual. He had that bad leg, after all, and sometimes it seemed he was having difficulty just getting through a hard practice.

But Muck was up the fence and over, his bad leg wiggling uncertainly for a moment as his skates hit the hard ice on the other side. The four figures came across the field to the rousing cheers of the Screech Owls, all of whom were now back on their feet and collecting their sticks.

Ty and Barry, both fine skaters who, as junior players, had for many years been coached by Muck Munro, were flying over the ice. Muck was coming slowly, businesslike. Mr. Dillinger, with his ankles bending terribly, was struggling, but even in the distance they could hear his high-pitched, uncontrolled laughter. Good old Mr. Dillinger. Game for anything. Any time.

Muck came up to the circle of Owls and stopped. He had his whistle around his neck. He blew it.

"Okay," he said. "You're loosened up. Let's work on a few drills."

"*Not a practice!*" Nish howled.

"And why not, Nishikawa?" Muck asked, looking sternly on his favourite target.

"They said on the radio that the rink was closed, everything cancelled."

Muck looked around, as if for the first time. "Rink looks fine to me, Nishikawa."

He blew his whistle again. "Okay, we have a big game against Orillia next Friday. I want to see some breakouts and sharp passing, understand?"

Travis could hear Nish sigh behind him: "Geez."

"Old crocks against young hotshots," Muck said, smiling now. "But we get Sarah's line and Jenny in net, okay?"

It took a moment for the announcement to sink in. Muck wanted to play! They had come to join in the shinny game! Travis felt a shiver go up his back. He had never seen Muck play before, only heard about him: the brilliant junior career, the shattered leg in the pile-up, the operation that didn't quite work, the end of Muck Munro's great dream of one day playing in the National Hockey League.

"ALLL-RIGHTTTT!" Nish screamed right into Travis's ear. Travis winced, but began shouting himself.

Travis and Sarah and Dmitri were lined up at centre, waiting for Data to flip the puck in the air between Sarah and Andy for the opening faceoff. Behind Travis, waiting with his stick perfectly poised on the ice like some old 1950s hockey card, was Muck. To Muck's side was Ty, then Barry, with Mr. Dillinger barely holding his balance behind them, and far behind them all, Jenny was kicking out her foam-rubber pads, ready.

Never had skating felt so sweet and fun. With no boards to consider, Travis could let his feet go where they wished. He could turn at will, skating backwards or forwards whenever he felt like it. Sarah picked up the puck, circled twice, and dropped it back to Muck, who took the pass perfectly and hit Travis with a single stride and a long, hard pass that sent him straight up the creek and free.

Muck's pass had felt different on Travis's stick. Strong, sure, accurate, it hit the blade so hard it nearly knocked the stick out of his hand.

An NHL pass. That was the phrase Muck always used when he talked to them about the importance of making sure passes got through, how accuracy and speed won hockey games, not soft passes that people had to slow for or reach for. Travis hadn't varied his speed a moment for the pass to arrive, perfectly.

Travis came in on Nish, his friend backing up wildly, laughing and pointing the blade of his stick at Travis's face, taunting him. Travis could hear skates sizzling up alongside him, then breaking away. Heavy skates – Ty in full flight. He flipped the puck, hoping Ty would catch it on the far side of Nish, and it worked perfectly. Ty was in alone, but without looking, he passed hard straight back down the ice, and the puck cracked hard and sure on another stick: Muck was coming straight through centre.

Nish turned back, still laughing, and lunged at the oncoming coach. Muck very casually slipped the puck through Nish's feet, and then, as he passed by, reached with his stick and dumped Nish flat on his back, sending him crashing into a stand of bulrushes.

Muck, a huge grin on his face now, snapped a wicked pass that shot under Travis's stick, past Ty, and hit Sarah coming in on the fly. The pass was so perfect it shot like a laser in a science-fiction movie. Sarah faked once, slid the puck across to Dmitri, and Dmitri tipped the puck into the side of the open net.

"*No fair!*" Nish was screaming. "*No fair! It doesn't count! I got dumped!*"

"What are you talking about?" Muck said as he tapped Sarah for her play.

"*You dumped me!*" Nish wailed.

"You fell over your own big feet, Nishikawa. Everyone saw what happened."

"*No way! You dumped me! Didn't he, Trav.*"

"Not that I saw," said Travis.

"Anybody see it?" asked Muck.

"Not me," said Ty.

"He fell," said Barry.

"Fell," said Data, who was on Nish's team.

Nish was spinning around, his face twisting in fury. He looked like he was going to explode. He screwed his eyes shut, then stared hard at Muck for a moment.

"I'll get you back for that," he vowed.

For another hour they played, until the sweat was rolling down their spines and their shirts and jackets and pants were damp. Mr. Dillinger's horseshoe of thin hair was soaking wet and there was sweat dripping off Muck's chin.

But no one – no one – was as wet as Nish, who played like he was possessed, carrying the puck, passing the puck, driving the net, trying always, without success, to dump Muck Munro whenever he came close.

"He can play this game when he wants to," Muck said after Nish made one magnificent rush that resulted in a pretty goal by Jesse Highboy.

Travis knew what Muck meant. You had to fire Nish up – bug him a little – to find the hockey player that was hidden inside. And nobody was better at firing him up than their coach, Muck Munro.

Muck blew his whistle, serious this time.

"I don't want anybody catching cold," he said. "Everyone head home now and change into something dry."

The Owls all groaned. No one wanted to quit. But everyone knew that Muck was right. It was time.

"This is the way the game was meant to be played," Muck said. "Good workout, all of you – even you, Nishikawa."

Travis looked at Nish, who was beaming through his sweat. Nish clearly knew he had put on a great performance, and he probably also knew how Muck had inspired it.

3

IN THE EVENING IT BEGAN TO SNOW. IT SNOWED hard, all through the night, and when Travis woke on Sunday morning, his bedroom window was covered with frost on the inside, and half covered with soft, pillowy snow piled up on the sill outside. The frost was beautiful. It looked like intricately painted white feathers.

With the back of his hand, Travis wiped away the icy feathers and looked out on the town. It seemed a world removed from the strange and beautiful landscape of the day before. Where yesterday had been hard as glass, today was soft and familiar as a quilt comforter: Tamarack under snow, the morning after a heavy fall.

And yet this day was just as different as the day before. Usually a big snowfall meant snowploughs and sanders and salt trucks working through the night, but today the streets were blocked. The heavy snowfall was like a throw rug over a newly waxed, slippery hardwood floor, dangerous to the step, nearly impossibly to plough.

Travis, yawning and scratching his sides, wandered into the kitchen. The radio was on low in the background, an announcer reading a long list of cancellations due to weather.

"There's a pot of porridge on," his mother said. "Cream of wheat – help yourself."

Travis began spooning the thick, sticky porridge into a bowl. His father was at the kitchen window. He was leaning over, craning to see past the bird feeder and into the sky.

"It's clouding over," he said. "I think we're in for more of it."

Nish telephoned in the early afternoon. Some of the other Owls were heading out to the hill over by the school, and Nish wanted Travis to bring some cardboard for them to slide on.

It turned out they hardly needed the hill. Travis, hanging onto two large sides cut from a cardboard box, virtually glided down River Street to Cedar, where Nish was waiting for him.

There were two perfect channels in the snow where Nish had slid across the intersection and landed, flat on his back, in the snowbank on the far side. He lay there, calmly picking up mittfuls of snow and dropping them into his open mouth as if they were juicy grapes.

"No school tomorrow," Nish announced as Travis came, slipping and sliding, to an uneasy stop beside him.

"How do you know?"

"No way they're going to get the streets cleared in time. My dad says they can't even get the trucks out onto the road."

"I liked it better yesterday," said Travis.

"So did I," agreed Nish. "Best winter's day in history."

Travis didn't bother to argue. Christmas was usually pretty good, and so was Travis's birthday, March 18. But he knew Nish's way of talking only too well. Everything was either the best thing that had ever happened, or the worst thing that had ever happened. In between didn't exist for Nish. In between, Travis smiled to himself, was where the rest of the world – the real world – lived.

They set off for the hill by the schoolyard, dragging their cardboard behind them. Data and Andy were already there and had their own supply of cardboard, which flattened the fresh snow against the ice below and made a slick, quick run that took them flying down the hill and right out across the schoolyard where, eventually, they came to a halt. Nish, with his extra weight – and, Andy claimed, a little bit of cheating – set a "New World Record" for distance, reaching the far side of the playground on one great run.

Slowly, the Owls gathered. Sarah and Jenny showed up together, followed by Liz. Jesse

Highboy came wearing a pair of mukluks from James Bay, soft rabbit-skin boots that let him slide so easily the rest of the Owls were able to stand in a circle in the schoolyard and send him skidding and bouncing back and forth like a pinball. Dmitri came, and Lars, Derek, Wilson, Jeremy, Simon – one by one they arrived until virtually the entire Screech Owls team was assembled at the schoolyard, the very place that next day most of them were hoping to avoid.

"A *new* New World Record!" Nish announced grandly from the top of the hill. "Guaranteed!"

Everyone stood back and watched him preparing to leap, like a belly-flopper, off the crest of the hill and onto the cardboard slide.

A car horn honked loudly.

"Thank you," Nish waved toward the car. "Thank you very much. Thank you."

The horn blew again.

"He's not honking at you!" Andy shouted. "He's stuck!"

Nish paid no attention. Presuming, as always, that the entire world was watching him, cheering him on, he leapt out into the air and landed, with a puff of light snow, on the top of the run.

The car horn honked again, longer this time.

"Let's see if we can push him out!" Jesse called to the rest of the Owls.

"C'mon!" called Jeremy.

"He shouldn't even be out," said Sarah as she caught up to Travis.

"I can't make out who it is," said Travis.

The car was almost completely covered in snow. The driver had dug a round hole through the snow on the windshield, but otherwise there was no way of seeing in or out. The back window was buried. The side windows were caked with snow.

"That's dangerous," said Sarah.

"Dangerous just to try driving in this," said Travis.

The driver's door opened, and the snow just above it on the roof broke off in a silent, white explosion, covering the red coat and hat attempting to emerge.

It was Mrs. Vanderhoof, an elderly woman from the apartments near the church. In a moment she was brushing away the snow from her coat and face and seemed, somehow, both frightened and excited at the same time.

"Well," she said in a grand, theatrical voice, "*that* was quite a ride!"

She was giggling and shaking at the same time.

"They haven't sanded the roads," said Sarah. "Cars can't get anywhere."

"I can see that, my dear," Mrs. Vanderhoof said indulgently. "I think I shall simply return home and wait for them to fix the streets properly. This wouldn't have happened, young lady, if my father were still the mayor of this poor town."

Mrs. Vanderhoof began getting back into her car. Sarah winked at Travis and went to work trying to clear off a better view for the old woman. She used her arms to sweep the windows clear, and some of the other Owls moved in to help.

Travis was amused by the way older people so often talked about *the way things used to be*. It seemed nothing was ever as good as the way things used to be. If he believed everything his parents and grandparents – and people like Mrs. Vanderhoof – told him, then surely the past had to be a world where the sun always shone, where no one ever had any money but everyone was far happier without it, where everyone was honest, where the cuts of meat were always better, where a pop cost a nickel, where people helped each other out, and, it seemed, where the moment a snowflake struck the ground, a sander was standing by to make sure no one slipped on it.

The automatic window on the driver's side groaned, then gave, and as it lowered, the snow it was supporting dropped away, sending a cloud of sparkling white in over Mrs. Vanderhoof's shoulder and face. She practically spit through the snow as she barked out her orders.

"You're going to have to push me out of here!" she commanded.

The Screech Owls crowded around the rear of the car where the wheels had caught in the heavier snow. Some of the kids pulled snow away with their arms. Others kicked it away with their boots.

"*New World Record! New World Record!*"

None of them even turned as Nish, red and sweating, came scrambling up the incline to where Mrs. Vanderhoof's car was marooned.

"I beat – my old – record by twenty – feet!" he puffed.

"Who cares?" Sarah said. "Get back there and push!"

Nish looked shocked at her lack of interest, but he hurried back to the rear of the car anyway, where the others were starting to push.

"I got a new world . . ." Nish began again.

But no one was listening.

"If we rock it enough," Andy was saying, "it'll come free."

"*Now!*" Data called. "*Now!*"

With Mrs. Vanderhoof gunning the engine, and the car wheels screaming as they spun and found nothing but ice, the Owls worked steadily, as a team. Finally, on one of Data's mighty yells, the car lifted free and slid out onto the road again, Mrs. Vanderhoof hauling the wheel the wrong way so the car almost spun right around.

"*One-eighty!*" Simon shouted. "*Go for it, Mrs. Vanderhoof!*"

"Go easy on the gas," Sarah told her through the open window. "Take it easy and we'll push."

Mrs. Vanderhoof nodded and gripped the wheel as if she were a fighter pilot about to drop down through the clouds. Sarah turned so she wouldn't laugh and hurried to rejoin the rest of the Owls preparing to push once more.

"*Easy, now!*" Sarah shouted ahead to Mrs. Vanderhoof.

Mrs. Vanderhoof listened. She eased off on the gas, and, with the Owls pushing hard, the tires found some grip on the ice and the car began moving, slowly, back up the street.

They pushed until the road flattened out near Mrs. Vanderhoof's apartment building. Travis was working hard, his eyes closed. When he opened them, he realized that Mrs. Vanderhoof's was the only vehicle out on the road. The way back to her apartment was absolutely clear but for her own winding tracks through the snow; no one else had been foolish enough to try the roads before they were ploughed and sanded.

This must have been the way it was in the days before they salted and sanded the roads, thought Travis. This must have been what roads were like when they used chains on the tires. He remembered his father laughing when he talked about "hitching" in the good old days.

Why not? Travis thought. *Why not?*

4

THE CAR WAS MOVING ON ITS OWN, NOW. MOST of the Owls had already let go as Mrs. Vanderhoof began gathering speed, the tires holding fairly well on the flat stretch.

"*Go!*" Nish called as he gave one last mighty push.

Travis was the last of them still hanging onto the car. He knew he, too, should push off. But he had to see what "hitching" felt like. He dropped down into a crouch, and grasped the bumper firmly.

He felt the ground rush under his feet; he was sliding along behind the car as if on air.

No wonder his father had compared it to waterskiing! Travis giggled as he felt the ice cobble of the road tickling the bottoms of his feet through his boot-soles. He was slipping along faster, now, the ground moving under him quickly and smoothly.

"TRAAA–VISSS! WHAT'RE YOU DOING?"

Travis giggled at the challenge in Nish's voice, the near anger. For once, Travis was the one misbehaving and Nish was acting sensibly.

He let go again with his right hand and waved.

Mrs. Vanderhoof slowed for the turn into her parking lot, and Travis dug hard, using the edges of his winter boots against the ice. The moment he felt them bite, he let go and flew on down the street, while Mrs. Vanderhoof, completely unaware that she had had a "hitcher," headed back into the safety of her parking lot.

Travis slid and slid, turning gracefully in his crouch as he travelled towards a waiting snowbank. He could hear the rest of the Owls, shouting and screaming as they chased after him.

"*Traaaaa-visssss!*"

"*YAY, TRAA-VISS!*"

There was no disapproval in Data's voice, or Andy's, or Jesse's, or even Sarah's. He could hear them all, running after him, as thrilled as he was by his father's old game of "hitching."

Nish was one of the first to reach Travis. Unlike the others, he seemed almost angry.

"*What're you doing?*"

"Hitching."

"*What?*"

"Hitching," Travis repeated.

"*What's that?*"

"My dad used to do it in the days before they salted and sanded the streets. He and his friends used to travel all over town that way."

"*They did?*" squealed Jenny. "*Neat!*"

"Awesome," said Simon.

"Some people do it on the country roads in Sweden," said Lars. "But it's against the law."

"It probably is here, too," said Travis. "Besides, you can't do it once the streets are salted. Your feet would catch and you'd go down face first."

"Sounds dangerous," said Sarah.

"Sounds *fun*," said Andy.

"Sounds *stupid*," said Nish.

"You're just jealous 'cause you weren't first," said Data, matter-of-factly.

No one else said anything. They all knew Data was right.

"*Let's go hitching!*" shouted Wilson.

"*Yeah!*"

"There's no other cars out," said Nish in a voice that would dampen spirits at a birthday party.

"Yes there is!" said Andy. "There goes one!"

There was indeed another car out, crawling slowly along the next street. It, too, had just a small spyhole cleared through the snow on the windshield, and another small hole on the window of the driver's side. Apart from that, the driver might as well have been in an army tank.

Before Travis could stop them, half of the Owls had broken away in a slipping, sliding run for the nearest intersection, where they waited for the car to ease down into a half stop and then "walk" through the turn onto River Street.

Andy was first to chase after the car and dip down to hitch onto the back bumper. Nish was second. The driver, his wing mirror caked in snow, his rear window buried, had no idea that they were there. They held tight, and the car swooshed them away over the frozen road.

The car turned again at Cedar Street, and both Andy and Nish let go, yelling and screaming as they used the turn to launch themselves off in a long, spinning freestyle ride farther down River Street. The others chased along, thrilled with their new game.

Travis felt a sudden burst of guilt. What if his father saw them? What if something happened?

But what could happen? The roads were smooth with ice, the banks were soft, enough snow had fallen to pad any falls, and the cars were barely creeping along.

They played past dark. They set up a system where a couple of Owls would struggle up the sliding hill by the school and spot cars daring to chance the slippery streets. A call that one was coming along Cedar would send a pack of Owls to the intersection, where they could hide until the driver – keeping his eyes fixed warily on the road ahead – had almost passed. Then they would scurry out, grab the bumper, and away. A call that a car was coming up River would send them in another direction.

"*Cedar!*" Andy called out from the hill.

Andy was doing hill duty with Travis, and in

the sweep of headlights as the car turned onto Cedar and headed for the intersection, Travis could see Owls scurrying. Data with his head down, Nish jumping and rolling behind cover.

Nish wasn't complaining now, Travis thought. Of course by now, Nish would believe he had invented the game. Soon he'd be claiming a "New World Record" for hanging on to bumpers.

The car slowed, and Nish and Data slipped out, grabbed the bumper, and were away down the street.

Travis was looking ahead of them up River. Headlights were approaching, bouncing from one bank to the other.

Another car was coming. *And this one was out of control!*

"*River!*" he shouted.

Andy immediately saw the danger.

"*They better ditch!*" Andy shouted.

"DITCH!" Travis yelled.

"BAIL OUT! BAIL OUT!" Andy called, cupping his hands around his mouth.

But it was no use; they couldn't hear.

The car was coming too fast! It slipped from side to side, the headlights running up the nearest snowbank and splashing out for a moment over the schoolyard and up the hill to Travis and Andy.

Travis began running down the hill, slipping and calling at the same time.

"NISHHHHHH!" he called. "DITCH!"

The driver pulling the two "hitchers" swung to avoid the fishtailing vehicle, and his quick yank of the steering wheel sent the rear of his car sliding out over the centre of the road.

With the sudden movement Data lost his grip. He flew out across the road, rolling, with Nish hurtling right behind him.

"DAAAA-TA!" Travis called.

Travis and Andy watched helplessly as a terrible scene unfolded below them. Both cars jammed on their brakes, the wheels locking and sliding, hopelessly, on the ice. Data and Nish seemed to float at first, still unaware of the danger they were flying into. And then Data raised his arms to cover his face.

There was no *crash*, no screaming, no crunching of metal or glass or, for that matter, bones.

Just a *whumphhhh!* The sound of a pillow swung against a wall.

Not even a cry.

And a second later, another soft thud, the sound of Nish hitting next, farther down the side.

Then the sound of one car going up on the bank, the snow and ice crunching it to a halt. The sound of the other car finally catching, the wheels coming to a halt.

And the sound of Travis's own voice, screaming, "NNNN-OOOOOOOOOOOOO!!"

5

TRAVIS WAS FIRST OVER THE SNOWBANK AND down onto the road. The driver who had, without knowing it, been towing the two boys was already out of his car, the door wide open and the interior light casting an eerie glow onto the scene.

Nish was lying flat on his back, moaning, holding his arm.

Data was lying to the side, halfway up the bank, his head pushed down against his shoulder. He was silent, as if sleeping.

"*What the hell's going on here?*" the first driver shouted. There was anger in his voice, mixed with concern.

The door of the other car popped open, and the pale light inside revealed a large figure, huddled over the steering wheel, in a thick woollen tuque pulled down low.

The second driver made an uncertain move to get out, his galoshes catching on something and kicking it free so that it jumped out the door and fell, ringing, on the icy road.

Travis and Andy had to skirt the second car to reach their friends. Travis was so close he could feel the heat rising from the open door. And he could smell something. Something strong.

Alcohol!

"*Nish!*" Travis called. "*Data!*"

Nish was moaning, twisting his body so he could cradle his arm. He was starting to cry. If Nish was crying, he had to be hurt.

But still Data was silent, not even moving.

Travis headed for Nish; Andy for Data. Andy dropped down onto his knees, almost spinning into their injured friend.

"DON'T TOUCH HIM!"

It was Sarah, screaming at the top of her lungs.

"ANDY, DON'T TOUCH HIM!"

Andy backed off as if Data were suddenly too hot to touch. Sarah's scream had such urgency to it, such sureness, that he scrambled out of the way as Sarah and Jenny and several of the other Owls arrived at the scene.

"*He mustn't be moved!*" Sarah shouted. "*Somebody call an ambulance!*"

The driver of the second car, the one that had hit the boys, was half out of his car. Travis looked up from where he was crouched beside Nish, who was starting to cry louder from the pain. Travis couldn't make out a face; all he saw was someone large and unsteady. Then suddenly the bulky figure dropped back into the car and slammed the door.

"I've got a cellphone," the first driver said. He hurried to his open door and reached in towards the passenger seat.

The engine of the second car roared. There was a loud clunk as the transmission was forced into gear. The car jumped slightly, and then the tires caught.

"*Look out!*" Andy called. "*He's moving!*"

Travis had to push Nish farther to the side, raising a terrible, blood-curdling shriek from Nish, who was in no condition to move.

"STOP! STOP!" Sarah screamed at the driver, half crying. "CAN'T YOU SEE THERE ARE PEOPLE HURT HERE?!"

But he would not stop. The car lurched, shuddered, slid again. The wheels sang hideously on the ice, and the car jerked away, the Screech Owls scattering in its path.

"*We need the police here, too!*" the first driver shouted into his cellphone. "*And hurry, please!*"

There was such desperation in the man's voice that Travis shuddered.

"STOP! . . . STOP! . . . PLEASE STOP, BEFORE YOU HURT SOMEONE ELSE!" Sarah screamed after the departing car. But it was useless. Sobbing now, Sarah sank to her knees in the snow-covered street.

Travis pulled her up, and as Sarah regained her feet, still sobbing, he helped brush off the snow.

"How's Nish?" she asked.

"His arm might be broken," Travis told her. "Are you okay?"

"I'm fine!" she said, starting to run back. "Come on, we've got to make sure no one moves Data! He's hurt bad." She sobbed again. "Really bad."

They turned together, holding on to each other. Travis could feel Sarah shaking through her heavy winter clothes. Car headlights danced over her face, showing not only tears, but also a fury Travis had never imagined possible in one so kind and mild as Sarah.

There were more headlights approaching.

And sirens.

The ambulance was here.

And right behind the ambulance, the police.

6

TRAVIS'S MOTHER AND FATHER SAT UP LATE WITH him that night. He'd tried to sleep, but couldn't. He lay in his bed and tried to turn his thoughts away from everything that had happened, but each time he was about to drop off to sleep, the day's events would swarm back into his head.

His father was on the telephone. Mr. Lindsay had called the police, the hospital, Muck, Mr. Cuthbertson, Nish's parents, Data's parents, the police again.

"It seems no one got the licence-plate number," he said at the end of this final call. His voice sounded tired, discouraged.

Travis was drinking hot chocolate. It seemed to lessen the sting in his throat, but he still didn't think he could talk without starting to cry.

"What about the car?" Mrs. Lindsay asked.

Mr. Lindsay shook his head. "No identification. There was so much snow over it, none of the kids could even tell what kind it was, let alone what colour."

"The man who stopped, didn't he see anything?"

Mr. Lindsay shook his head sadly. "It was Art Desmond. The real-estate guy. He was using his cellphone when the other guy drove off. He didn't even get a look."

The police wanted to come around and talk to Travis in the morning. He wouldn't, after all, be going to school, but this was hardly the day off he and Nish and Data and the rest had imagined. Travis had no idea what he could tell them. He hadn't seen the driver's face. It was too dark, and his tuque had been pulled down too low.

Nish's parents telephoned from the hospital. Nish had a broken wrist, but apparently it had set easily. He'd have to wear a cast for four to six weeks.

"Then he'll be as good as ever," Mr. Lindsay explained.

Good as ever? Travis wondered. *Nish?* He was tempted to make a little joke, but the impulse quickly died.

The news about Data wasn't as promising.

"He's still in surgery," Mr. Lindsay said.

Two police officers came to the house to interview Travis. One was a young woman, who was very concerned about how he felt. The other was an older man, who acted almost as if the Owls were the real criminals here. Twice he told Travis they could be arrested for "hitching." Twice Travis told him they'd never do it again. He wished the policeman would believe him; he had never been more serious about anything.

They went over the facts again, but they didn't add up to much. Travis couldn't think of anything to help in their search for the missing driver.

"There was a bottle found at the scene," said the woman officer.

"What sort of bottle?" Mr. Lindsay asked.

"Seagram's V.O. rye whisky, thirteen-ounce – commonly known as a mickey," the policewoman answered. "Empty."

"I think I heard something fall out of the car," said Travis.

"You're certain of that, son," the older officer said sternly.

"Yes," Travis said.

"There must be fingerprints on the bottle," Mrs. Lindsay suggested.

The older officer looked at her quickly. "Fingerprints only mean something if you have someone you can match them to, ma'am," he said. "Besides, he was probably wearing gloves. It was cold that day."

"We can't even be absolutely certain it was his bottle," said the younger officer with a sad look.

"I think I smelled it," said Travis.

Both police officers turned back to Travis, keenly interested.

"Smelled what?" the older officer demanded.

"When he opened the door," Travis said, "this strong smell came out. I thought it was alcohol."

"You know what alcohol smells like?" the older officer asked.

"I think so."

"*Think so* isn't good enough," the officer said. "Would you be confident enough to tell a judge and a full courtroom that you smelled alcohol?"

"Before we get to court," Mr. Lindsay cut in, "you're going to have to come up with a suspect, aren't you?"

The older officer looked up, as if challenged. "That's fairly obvious, sir."

"And have you?"

"Have we what, sir?"

"Have you come up with a suspect."

"Not so far. No."

Around noon they got word about Data. One of the bones at the base of Data's neck had been broken in the accident, but the surgery had gone well. He had been fitted with a thick wire "halo" around his head to keep his neck absolutely still. It was attached by screws that had been planted into his skull, and rested on his shoulders.

Travis shuddered when he heard this. A "halo" suggested good behaviour, but they had been doing something terribly foolish – and it had all been started by Travis.

Travis was feeling desperately sorry for himself when the telephone rang again.

"It's for you, son," his father said, handing the receiver across the table.

"Hello?" Travis said uncertainly.

"It's Muck," a deep voice announced.

"You're our team captain, Travis," Muck said. "I want you to make the calls. I want the whole team at the hospital at five o'clock. Understand?"

"Y-yes," Travis said, uneasily.

"We're going to see Data," Muck said.

"Is it all right?" Travis asked.

"Yes, it's all right. He's asked for the whole team," said Muck. "Are you okay?"

Travis knew he wasn't. "I guess," he said.

"Be there," Muck said. "And be captain, okay?"

Travis knew what Muck meant. He wanted Travis to make sure the visit went right. Muck would expect the same if they were down two goals in an important game: no matter how they might feel inside, the Owls had to believe things would work out, that in the end they would succeed together as a team.

"Okay," Travis said.

7

THE OWLS GATHERED ON THE THIRD FLOOR OF the hospital. Most of them had brought gifts. Sarah was going to give Data the old teddy bear she usually kept hidden away in a pocket of her hockey bag. Andy had a copy of *The Hockey News*. Jesse had a beautiful dream catcher that he wanted to hang from Data's window to keep away the bad dreams and let in the good ones. Dmitri had a hockey cap from Moscow Dynamo that his cousin, Slava, had given him.

Even Nish was there, holding out his cast as if it were some kind of medal for bravery.

"It's not plaster," he said. "It's some new kind of plastic they developed for space missions. I might even be able to play with it on."

Nish's eyes were both black from hitting head first into the side of the car the drunk had been driving.

"You look like you were in a fight with Tie Domi," Sarah teased.

"I was," Nish shot back. "And if you think I look bad, you should see him. They got him in a room down the hall. He can't walk or talk yet."

It would take more than a couple of black eyes and a broken wrist to shut up Nish.

"Here come Data's parents!" Jenny whispered urgently.

The Owls fell silent. Mr. and Mrs. Ulmar and their daughter, Julie, came down the hall and turned into the reception area. They looked drained and beaten. But Mrs. Ulmar managed a smile. As soon as she saw them, she walked up and gave Nish a hug. Nish hugged back, using one hand, and turned beet-red.

"Larry's glad you came," she said. "He's waiting for you."

"You – look – like – a – raccoon," Data said when he saw Nish.

"You look like an angel," Nish shot back.

"Not – yet," Data said, a weak smile forming. "Not – for – a – long – time . . . I – hope."

They gathered in a group around the bed. Data lay on his back, completely still, the halo preventing any motion of his head and neck. It was as if they were staring down at a stranger, not their friend. Travis felt nervous; he didn't know how to act. Everyone had noticed the way Data spoke, each word like a sentence on its own.

Sarah took charge. She walked to the head of the bed, then kissed her fingertips and gently placed the kiss on her friend's cheek.

"I brought you someone to keep you company," she said, holding up the bear.

Data couldn't turn his head to look, but his eyes moved down so he could see.

"Thanks," he said.

One by one, the others went up with their gifts and their hellos, and Data seemed pleased each one of them had come.

"Do the screws hurt?" Fahd asked when it was his turn.

"Only – when – I – do – somersaults," said Data.

Everyone laughed, and it felt, to Travis, like a magic remedy had just taken away the sick feeling in the pit of his stomach. It was still Data, good old Data.

"What can you feel?" Nish asked.

Travis winced. Like Fahd's question about the screws, this was something everyone wanted to know but no one else had dared to ask.

"Not – much," said Data. "The – doctor – can't – tell – how – much – feeling – will – come – back."

"Will you be able to play again this year?" Fahd asked. The answer to that one was obvious, and as Fahd's question hung in the air, they all wished he hadn't asked it.

Data shut his eyes. He couldn't shake his head to say no. He had to say it out loud.

"I – I guess – not," he finally said.

ON FRIDAY NIGHT, THE SCREECH OWLS PLAYED
at home against Orillia. Mr. Lindsay drove Travis
down to the rink, as usual, but for once neither
father nor son said a word. Travis had never felt
less like playing a hockey game in his life.

When he reached the dressing-room door, he
thought, at first, he must be early. Normally, as
soon as the door was open just a crack, he would
be greeted by the squeals and shouts of the Owls
getting dressed for a game. But this time, as he
shifted his bag and sticks off his shoulder and
backed in through the dressing-room door, there
was no sound from inside.

And yet the dressing room was half full. Sarah
was there, already dressed but for her skates and
sweater. Fahd was there. And Lars, sitting quietly
with his Owls sweater hanging above him. Mr.
Dillinger was busy at the back of the room,
sharpening Sarah's skates.

Travis came in and set his bag quietly on the
floor. He rested his sticks against the wall and
moved to his own seat. Still, no one had said a
word. He looked over at Sarah, who was biting

her lip. She pointed back at her sweater. She wanted him to see something.

Travis looked at his own sweater, number 7, hanging at the back of his stall. There was a new little crest sewn on it over the heart, just to the side of his *C*. It was a small four-leafed clover, with the number 6 in the centre.

Data's number.

Travis looked back at Sarah, who jerked her thumb towards Mr. Dillinger, busy as ever at his sharpening machine. Of course, Mr. Dillinger would have had the crests made, would have stitched them on himself and hung the sweaters up without a word. Good old Mr. Dillinger.

Soon the team was all there, each player entering in silence, then sitting in silence. Some even with their helmets pulled on. There were two sweaters still hanging up untouched. Data's number 6, of course, but also number 3: Nish.

Still no one had said a word.

The door opened and Muck came in. And right behind Muck – with his arm in a sling poking out through the opened zipper of his Screech Owls jacket – was Nish. Nish's cast had a green four-leafed clover painted on it, with a number 6 in the middle.

"We have a new assistant coach, tonight," Muck announced.

Nish beamed from ear to ear and took a

ridiculous bow in Sarah's direction. Sarah rolled her eyes.

"And we have another one who can't be with us," Muck added.

He said nothing else, just turned and walked out, staring straight ahead. For once, Fahd didn't have to ask the obvious: who? It was Data – tonight the Screech Owls were playing for Data.

"*Let's go!*" Sarah suddenly shouted, jumping up and pumping a gloved fist in the air. She grabbed her stick from the wall and slammed it, hard, into Jenny's big goalie pads.

"*Stone 'em, Jen!*" Sarah shouted.

"*Let's do it for Data!*" Andy called.

"*For Data!*" Lars yelled.

"*Data!*"

"*Data!*"

"*And Nish!*" someone called.

Travis turned to look. It was Nish calling for himself.

Nish shrugged sheepishly, and Travis smiled. He swung his sticks back as he plucked them from the wall, and tapped his good friend lightly on the shins.

"For Data *and* Nish," he said.

What was it about this game of hockey, Travis wondered, that sometimes everything could feel wrong – even the way your feet fit into the skates

– and a day later everything could feel exactly right? He felt this Friday night as if skating had somehow become the natural way of human movement. He felt as if the ice were at his mercy; he was in no danger of slippery corners or too great a distance. If he reached for the puck, it seemed to reach back for him, puck and stick blade seemingly magnetized. He put his first two warm-up shots off the crossbar.

Muck and Nish and Barry worked the bench. Ty was out of town, so Nish pretty much handled the defence on his own, taking signals from Muck and using his good arm to tap the backs of sweaters to indicate line changes.

When Sarah's line was out, Muck wanted Sarah to go in hard with one winger on the fore-check and try to stop the good Orillia defence before they could get out of their own end with the puck. The other winger was to lie back around the blueline, hoping to intercept any pass that Sarah and the other winger might force.

Travis was first in on the top Orillia defence-man, and he came in hard, skating as well as, if not better than, he'd ever skated before. Was it because of their day of shinny in the open creek? Was it because of Data? He didn't know; all he knew was that as soon as he saw where he needed to be, he was there. He flew into the Orillia end, racing towards the other team's best puck-handler. He had no idea how he knew, just that he knew. He came in hard and then dragged his right skate just as the defender tried to slip the puck between Travis's feet. The puck caught, and Travis, instantly, came free with it on the other side.

He kicked the puck up onto his stick, dug hard to turn towards the net, and then deked back again to the near side of the net, forcing the Orillia goalie to shift tight to his post. A quick little pass across the crease and Sarah had buried the puck with a quick snap of a shot.

First shift, and the Owls had already scored.

The Owls on the ice mobbed Sarah but she shook them free. She hurried to where the linesman was digging the puck out and held out her glove for it. He handed it over with a smile. Perhaps he thought it was her first-ever goal.

"For Data," Sarah said when she got back to the bench.

She handed the puck to Nish to hold for her. Nish took the puck in his good hand and jammed it into his pocket.

"*Ouch!*" Nish yelped, and yanked his hand out, fast. His thumb had caught on something. It was already beading blood.

Mr. Dillinger quickly grabbed a towel to press against the cut. He dabbed quickly and looked carefully at the damage.

"Not deep," he said. "I'll get a bandage."

Travis's line was back out for another shift. When they got back, Mr. Dillinger was just finishing up. With the scissors he carried on his belt, he snipped off the last wrap of bandage.

"Great!" Nish said. "Now I've got *no* hands!"

If they thought the game against Orillia would be easy, they were wrong. The Owls had scored first, but the Orillia goalie had no intention of letting in any more goals after Sarah's.

Travis had rarely worked harder in a game. He skated well and had plenty of good chances, but it was as if a huge plywood board had been nailed over the other team's net. He was robbed twice on glove saves. Dmitri failed on two breakaways.

Something was wrong with Owls. They were giving fine individual efforts, but they weren't working like a team. Travis thought it was as though they were missing something – and then he shut his eyes and shook his head hard.

They *were* missing something: *Data*.

Inspired by their goaltender, the Orillia players slowly mounted their comeback. Playing magnificently – everyone working together – they tied the game in the second period and went ahead, to stay, early in the third. Muck pulled Jenny in the final minute, but even with an extra attacker the Owls could not get past the splendid Orillia goalie.

The game over, the Screech Owls headed for their dressing room in silence, heads down. Travis felt he had failed Data even more than he had failed the team. They had wanted to take him a win, but instead they had lost, and Orillia were now the top team in their division.

But at least they had the puck from Sarah's one goal. It wasn't much, but it was something to take to Data.

Sarah asked for Data's puck, and Mr. Dillinger had to reach into Nish's jacket pocket to get it.

"Watch your hand," Nish warned, holding out his bandaged thumb as proof of the danger.

"Okay," Mr. Dillinger said, "I got it."

Mr. Dillinger carefully pulled out the prized puck and flipped it to Sarah, who caught it easily.

But Mr. Dillinger wanted to find out what it was that had cut Nish's fingers.

"You've got something caught in here, son," he called.

Carefully, Mr. Dillinger pulled a sliver of shiny metal out of Nish's pocket.

"That's what I cut my hand on!" Nish shouted.

Mr. Dillinger blinked at the piece of chrome, turning it over and over. He handed it to Muck, who took it and carefully looked himself.

"Looks like a piece of trim," Muck said.

"Off a car," Mr. Dillinger said.

Nish shot a surprised and excited look at Travis.

A clue.

IT TOOK TWO DAYS FOR THE POLICE LABORATORY in Toronto to report back on the piece of metal that had turned up in Nish's pocket. It was side stripping from a car, all right. The car would have been a Chevrolet, but there were two different models it might have come from, and those models had been in production for three years. In other words, there were tens of thousands of cars the piece of metal could have come from. Dozens around Tamarack alone.

"They say the car might not even have come from here," Mr. Lindsay told Travis and Nish.

Travis sighed deeply. "What are they going to do?" he asked.

"They'll check similar cars in the area," Mr. Lindsay said, "see if one of them's missing some stripping from up around the front left side – but don't get your hopes up too high, boys. Travis's grandfather drives a Chevrolet. So does Mr. Dillinger. It's almost too common a model to do us any good."

Travis and Nish tried to play video games to pass the rest of the day, but Nish claimed he couldn't play up to his usual high standards with a cast on, and after a while they simply paused the game and talked.

"It can't be from out of town," Travis said.

"How do you know?" asked Nish. "It could have been driven here from anywhere. It's a *car*, after all."

"Yeah, but don't forget the day. It was so slippery, cars couldn't get anywhere. No one would drive any distance that day."

Nish was only half listening. "Maybe."

"And don't forget where he was. The back streets. No one would drive up here from Orillia or someplace like that and be driving around our back streets drunk, would they?"

"Probably not – but who knows what a drunk will do?"

"And that's significant, too," Travis almost shouted. He was excited; his brain was really working.

"What's significant?"

"He was drunk."

"Obviously."

"But he had to *get* drunk first."

"Obviously again."

"So, think of the direction he was headed."

Nish thought for a moment. "Towards Main Street, I guess."

"*Exactly!* Which means he was coming from . . . ?"

Nish looked at Travis, bewildered. "I don't know. There's nothing much up Cedar beyond the curling rink and the baseball diamonds. . . . Mr. Turley's farm . . . a few houses on the other side of the road . . ."

"An out-of-towner wouldn't come along that way. But somebody who lives up here would. Or maybe somebody who was at the curling rink, drinking."

"There was a bottle that fell out, remember. He didn't have to go to the curling rink to get drunk."

"Yeah, you're right. But maybe it was an old bottle, already empty. Or maybe he was already drunk and then continued drinking in his car. There's a good chance he was either someone from around here, maybe even up Cedar Street, or someone who'd been at the curling rink."

"That's not much to go on," said Nish, unimpressed.

"But we have something else," Travis protested.

"What's that?"

"The Chevrolet. We can find out who drives one who also lives out that way. Maybe even who has one and belongs to the curling club."

"Didn't you listen to your father?" Nish said, absentmindedly. "He said there were dozens of them."

"There are," said Travis, grinning with satisfaction. "But only one is missing a strip of metal."

Nish looked back at Travis, finally prepared to admit Travis might be right. "Let's get some help," he said.

They raised whatever Owls could be located quickly by telephone calls and knocking on doors. Sarah was there. And Jenny, Lars, Andy, Fahd, Dmitri, and Liz. Travis outlined what it was they were looking for: a mid-sized Chevrolet at least three years old but no more than six years old, colour uncertain.

"I can't tell one car from another," said Sarah.

"Don't worry," said Travis, "we can wipe off the snow until we see if it's a Chevrolet or not. And if it is, it'll just take a second to check the driver's side near the front for missing stripping. That should be simple enough."

They marked out an area of approximately six blocks, plus the curling rink, plus the new houses across from Turley's farm. Then, setting out in pairs, they arranged to meet back at the curling rink in an hour.

Travis and Nish found two Chevrolets that fit the description, but one was Travis's own grand-father's – and Harold Lindsay had never touched a drop of drink in his life – and the other was in perfect shape, its stripping as good as new. Sarah and Liz found three. One of them had a bashed-in side, but the damage was on the passenger side. The other two were in perfect shape, trim intact. Andy and Dmitri found only one, but it belonged to Mr. Dickens, who owned the Shell station at the corner of River and Main and who had coached most of the Screech Owls in atom. Like Travis's grandfather, he was one of the most respected men in town, and anyway, there was no damage on his car. Jenny and Fahd found none.

Six cars, and no suspects. But they still had the curling-rink parking lot to do.

"What if someone catches us?" asked Fahd, who was always worried about something.

"We'll pretend we're having a snowball fight," suggested Sarah. "Get your snow off the backs of the cars – that way you can check the make out."

"No fair!" complained Nish. "I can't pack."

Sarah rolled her eyes. "It is not a *real* snowball fight, Nishikawa. We are *pre-tend-ing*."

Sarah's idea worked brilliantly. They packed snowballs and checked for Chevrolets. They ducked down and, while they were hidden between cars, checked for missing metal stripping. One man even came out of the curling rink, saw them, and started laughing at their game. Little did he know he had just walked into the middle of a criminal investigation.

Finally the Owls had worked their way through all the rows and all the cars. They were snow-covered and exhausted.

"Four Chevrolets," said Travis, summing up, after they had all reported.

"And nothing missing," said Andy, dejected.

"Well . . . ," mumbled Fahd, seeming to search for the right words.

"You found something?" Travis asked.

"Not really, but —"

"But what?" Nish said impatiently.

"I think we need to look at one of them again," said Fahd.

He led the seven other Owls along one of the rows of cars, dipped between two of them, and in the next row found the one he wanted.

Andy checked carefully along the driver's side.

"It's in perfect shape," he announced.

"But," said Fahd, swallowing, "that's the point."

"*What*'s the point?" Nish asked in a challenging voice.

"It . . . it's *too* perfect," Fahd mumbled. "This is not a new car."

They all leaned closer around Andy. Travis took his glove off and rubbed it along the side of the car. Andy knocked the snow off further along. He wiped the metal clean, so it shone.

"This guy's had bodywork done," said Andy.

"And recently, too," said Travis.

"We've got something," said Sarah.

A second clue.

10

ALL EIGHT SCREECH OWLS SCRAMBLED UP AND over the high snowbank at the end of the lot. They lay on their stomachs, watched, and waited.

"I gotta be in by nine," Fahd warned.

"I'm good till nine-thirty," said Sarah.

"Nine."

"Nine-thirty."

"Nine."

"Nine."

"Nine."

"Midnight."

Travis turned to his side and looked crossly at Nish, who was beaming from ear to ear. Nish, the Man About Town, who would tell them he and his father sometimes enjoyed a good cigar after dinner. Who once maintained he'd driven the car around the block. Who in his imagination would stay up all night long, drinking and smoking and partying, but who would wake up in his Toronto Maple Leafs pyjamas in the morning and expect his mother to bring him in a bowlful of Fruit Loops while he watched the Saturday-morning cartoons.

"In your dreams," Sarah said.

How late they could all stay mattered. What if this really was the car they were looking for, and what if the driver was going to be curling and drinking until midnight? Would Nish still be on watch for him? Whoever it was who drove this Chevrolet with the new bodywork, he had to come out before the Owls went to bed.

They waited and talked. About the loss to Orillia. About the team. About Data. Strangely, though they couldn't help thinking about Data, none of them wanted to talk about him for long. Someone would say something about how well he was doing — how he could sit in a wheelchair now and was learning to drive it with his right hand, which he could move a little — but then, just as quickly, someone else would change the subject.

"I signed up for the Mock Disaster," announced Fahd.

"You *are* a disaster," said Nish.

"What is it?" asked Travis.

Fahd told them that Mrs. Wheeler's class had volunteered to work on an emergency drill the fire department and the hospital were putting on. It was basic training for the ambulance drivers and emergency-room hospital staff. They were going to simulate a bus accident, and some of the kids from school were going to be made up to look like they'd been injured in the wreck.

"I'm doing fake blood and broken bones," said Fahd. "It's fantastic!"

"Only *you* would think so," said Sarah, clearly relieved she wasn't in Mrs. Wheeler's class.

"*Look!*"

It was Lars's voice, low and urgent. The Owls shut up immediately and turned flat on their stomachs to peer over the bank. There was a large man moving out among the parked cars, headed in the general direction of the Chevrolet.

"*It's Booker!*" hissed Nish.

Booker? It took several moments before the name registered on Travis. Of course, Mr. Booker had once come out to help Muck with the early-season assessments, but he had been so foul-mouthed on the ice Muck had ordered him off and told him to go home. This was minor hockey, Muck told him, not the military.

The hockey association kept Mr. Booker away from coaching, but thought he'd do no harm as a team manager. They'd been wrong. Even in house league he'd been thrown out of games for abusing the referees, and finally he was banned altogether after he grabbed an opposing player by the scruff of the neck and pinned him to the arena wall when the two teams had left the ice. The player had tripped one of Mr. Booker's players during the game, but as Mr. Lindsay had explained to Travis later that night, tripping is a penalty, holding a kid by his throat against a wall is assault. Mr. Booker's career in hockey was over.

"*He's heading for it!*" hissed Andy.

They watched as Mr. Booker twisted his way through the cars towards the Chevrolet. He was fumbling in his pocket. He dropped something – keys, probably – and swore loudly as he bent to pick them up.

"Charming," said Sarah.

"He's drunk," said Lars.

Mr. Booker came up with the keys and fumbled with them at the door. Soon the interior light of the car came on as the door cracked open and they could see him getting in. He closed the door, started the car, and let the windshield wipers shake off the light dusting of snow that had fallen since he'd arrived. He sat a moment, letting the engine warm the windshield. Then his headlights came on, and they could hear the crunch of tires on the snow as he moved slowly out of the parking lot.

"Where does he live?" said Fahd.

"I don't have a clue," said Travis.

"I do," said Liz. "My mom and Mrs. Booker are friends."

"Where, then?" said Nish.

"Across from the farm. At the very end of Cedar."

"*Yes!*" Travis said.

The quickest route from the curling rink to the end of Cedar Street passed through the intersection where Data had been struck.

Booker would have been going home! Just like this, drunk, from the curling rink!

They had a third clue.

11

ON SUNDAY, THE SCREECH OWLS PRACTISED AT
noon – Nish skating, but unable to shoot – and
afterwards Muck asked the team to assemble again
at the hospital in an hour. They were going to
visit Data.

When the Owls got there, they found Data's
doorway almost blocked with other patients
trying to look inside. There were even a couple of
doctors on tiptoe trying to get a peek over the
crowd. The fact that the doctors weren't pushing
their way through to get to Data and were smiling
told Travis there was nothing to worry about.

Everyone made room to let the Owls pass
through, single file. There were more people in
the room, doctors and nurses, and a man in a blue
suit leaning over Data's bed. The man had dark
curly hair that was turning grey. *Who was it?*

Whoever he was, he looked up when Muck
came in and shook his hand warmly. Muck looked
sheepish, but the man seemed delighted, as if
running into an old friend he'd been missing.
Travis was no closer to guessing who the man
was, but he did look oddly familiar.

Muck turned to the small crowd around Data's bed, and everyone went even quieter than they had been.

"This, here, is Paul Henderson," he said.

Paul Henderson! *Of course!* Travis had a special coin at home with Paul Henderson on it. He had a sheet of stamps with Paul Henderson on them that he had put away. Paul Henderson, hero of the 1972 Summit Series, the man who had scored the winning goal for Canada against the Soviets with thirty-four seconds left in the final game. The most famous goal in hockey history.

"How ya doing, boys?" Paul Henderson said, then caught himself, seeing Sarah and Liz off to one side, Jenny and Chantal on the other. "And girls? Good, good, the Screech Owls are a truly modern team, I see."

"Mr. Henderson has something to announce," Muck said.

"Well, actually it's something Larry — sorry, *Data* — and I would both like to announce," said Paul Henderson. He turned, smiling, towards Data.

"We're going to play a game!" Data said from his bed. His voice sounded surprisingly strong.

"I proposed to Data that I bring a team of NHL old-timers up to Tamarack for a match. Muck's lined up the Flying Fathers to play against us. They're a bunch of priests who happen to play hockey — some of them pretty darn good — and they put on a great show. So — whadya say to that?"

"Go for it!" shouted Nish.

"Yes!" shouted Andy.

"*Shhhhh*," cautioned Sarah, reminding them where they were.

"Data, here, is going to need a few things," said Paul Henderson. "We want him to have the best wheelchair money can buy. And we want to get him a special computer so he can get back to school. And his parents are going to need a special van so they can get him to hockey games and the like."

Travis glanced quickly at Sarah, who smiled back. Travis wondered if Paul Henderson should even be talking about such things. But then, Data was already making unbelievable progress. The halo was gone, the small wounds where the screws had been tightened right into his skull were healing well. Best of all, he was getting some feeling and movement back in his shoulders, and he could move his right arm, though he had trouble gripping with his hand.

There was still nothing, however — no feeling at all — from Data's chest on down. The doctors said it likely wouldn't come back, and unless science one day figured out how to repair spinal cords, Data was never going to walk again.

"How did you find out about Data?" Fahd asked Paul Henderson. They were all wondering the same thing, but no one but Fahd would dare ask.

Paul Henderson smiled at Muck, who was standing in the far corner of the room, trying to avoid any attention.

"From my old friend, Muck. My old *winger*, I guess I should say."

Winger? As in *hockey* winger? Muck seemed to be blushing.

"Muck played with *you*?" Fahd asked.

"*I* played with Muck," Paul Henderson laughed. "We were on the same line in Kitchener."

Every face in the room, including Data's, was now turned towards Muck, who seemed to wish he could vanish into the wall. Every one of them was looking at Muck as if they'd never seen him before. He *played* with Paul Henderson?

"Was he any good?" Fahd asked.

"*A lot better than me!*" Paul Henderson laughed. "Maybe if you hadn't busted that leg so bad, Muck, you'd have scored that goal in Moscow."

"I'd've missed the net," Muck muttered.

Then Muck cleared his throat, changing the subject. "Let's clear this room so Data can get some rest now, okay?"

12

SO MUCH HAD HAPPENED. THE LARRY ULMAR Fundraising Game was scheduled for the first Sunday afternoon of the new month. The Flying Fathers were coming, complete with their hockey-playing *horse*. Paul Henderson had lined up some of the greatest names that ever played for the Toronto Maple Leafs, including Eddie Shack, Darryl Sittler, Lanny McDonald, and Frank Mahovlich. And right after the big game, the Screech Owls themselves were going to play, a return match against Orillia – another chance to get the win they'd so desperately wanted for Data.

The *Toronto Star* and the *Sun* and the *Globe and Mail* were all sending reporters and photographers. The Sports Network was coming to do a documentary on the charity work of the Flying Fathers. And Nish was getting a new cast.

"It's plastic and has a zipper," he told Travis. "I can take it off and put it on. Once the doctor says I can start playing again, I can use it just for games until the wrist heals completely. I'll be back sooner than anybody thinks."

Everything seemed to be going well – except the investigation.

The police were getting nowhere.

⬤

"Garbage night," Travis said to Nish.

"Huh?"

"Tonight's garbage night."

"Don't look at me – I can't lift a thing with this wrist!"

Travis shook his head. "I'm thinking about what *other* people put out."

"Whatdya mean?"

"We know what the guy who hit Data drinks, don't we? Seagram's V.O. whisky."

"Yeah. So?"

"So we check out Booker's recycling bin. See if that's what he drinks."

Nish thought about it a while. Finally he looked at Travis and smiled. "Good idea. Let's check it out."

Travis told his parents he was taking his geography notes over to Nish, which was true enough – only Nish told his parents he was headed over to Travis's to borrow the same notes. They met at the corner of Cedar and River, where Travis handed over the notes. Nish stuffed them into his backpack, and they set off for the neighbourhood where Mr. Booker lived.

It was a beautiful clear evening, already dark and very cold. Some houses already had their garbage out, in green plastic bags and blue recycling boxes for bottles and cans.

"Evening, boys!" a voice called across the road.

Travis and Nish turned to see Mr. Dickens, the old coach, set down two heavy garbage bags. He was clapping his bare hands together and rubbing them as he walked towards the boys.

"Hi, Mr. Dickens," said Travis.

"How's it going?" said Nish, who always talked the same, no matter whether he was speaking to a toddler or someone's grandmother.

Mr. Dickens stomped his feet and stabbed his hands deep into his pockets. "What do you young men hear from the hospital?" he asked.

"Data's doing pretty good," Nish said.

"He's moving around in a chair," said Travis.

Mr. Dickens seemed disappointed. "Then it's true what we hear: he won't walk again?"

"I guess not," said Nish. "Muck says it'd take a miracle."

"*Damn it!*" Mr. Dickens said, swallowing. He smiled. "Sorry, boys – I can't help it."

"Everybody's upset," said Travis. "Data's handling it better than anyone, to tell you the truth. You should go see him."

"Yeah," added Nish. "You used to coach the Data, didn't you?"

Mr. Dickens tried to speak, choked slightly, then cleared his throat. When he spoke, his voice was thin, breaking. "I'll pay him a visit, boys, I will. You tell him his old coach was asking after him, okay?"

"Sure, Mr. Dickens," said Travis.

Mr. Dickens looked at them. Travis could tell how much the old coach was bothered. It could have been the cold, but his eyes were damp, and he looked so sad, so upset. Like them, he was helpless to do anything about what had happened.

"Thanks, boys," he said.

Mr. Dickens turned and headed back, his boots slipping on the hard, slick snow cover. He nearly went down, caught himself, and walked back towards his garage to bring out the rest of his garbage.

"Need any help?" Travis asked.

"*No!*" Mr. Dickens said sharply. "No thanks."

He didn't look back.

Travis was pretty sure he knew why. Mr. Dickens didn't want them to see how upset he was about poor Data.

Booker lived a few blocks farther north, down a dead-end street called Poplar. There was a street-light at the corner, but no other lights apart from the houses. This was both good and bad. Good, because the dark gave them cover; bad, because they could barely see.

"I wish the moon was full," whispered Nish.

They were trying to walk quietly, taking soft steps so their boots wouldn't crunch in the snow.

"That's it – up there!" Travis whispered.

He pointed – despite being unable even to see his own hand – up towards a small one-storey wood-frame house with two dim lights attached to the side. One cast a dull glow over the front door; the other was at the near corner of the little house, barely illuminating the driveway.

"Good," said Travis. "He's already put his garbage out."

It was dark, but in the poor light from the house they could make out the dark shapes of two green garbage bags at the end of the drive-way. Beside the bags was a single dark box.

The two moved towards the snowbank closest to Booker's driveway.

"No car!" Travis whispered.

"Maybe he's at the curling rink," said Nish, hopefully.

"Maybe."

"Let's do it fast," said Nish.

Travis moved to the edge of the driveway, peeking around the high shovelled bank. He could see the recycling box. He could see the thin glow of the house lights dancing on glass.

There were bottles in it – lots of bottles!

"*Go!*" Nish hissed from behind him.

Travis took a deep breath. He hunched down, then darted across the front of the driveway, from one bank to the next. He stopped to gather his breath. His heart was pounding. He was sweating. Travis Lindsay, who hardly ever sweated during a game, was sweating now in the freezing cold of a black winter's night.

One deep breath and Travis darted into Booker's driveway. Crouching down, he hurried over to the recycling box.

He'd been right; it was full of bottles.

As he reached down into the box, his glove brushed one of the bottles on top, which slid down from the pile and clinked hard against more glass below.

"*Hurry!*" Nish hissed from the distance.

Travis reached into the bin and pulled a bottle out by the neck. He couldn't read the label, but he knew from the smell it was liquor.

Nish's voice cut through the still night air.

"CAR!"

No! Travis thought. *Not a car! Not now!*

He ducked down instinctively, just as the car's headlights swept over the tops of the banks and washed along the side of Booker's house.

But Nish must have panicked. Instead of sticking fast to the bank where he was hiding, he tried to come around it into the shelter of the driveway, where Travis was crouched out of sight.

His timing couldn't have been worse. As the car began to turn into Booker's driveway, Nish ran out into the glare of its headlights, and like a frightened deer stopped dead, petrified.

They could hear the whirr of an automatic window as the car came to a stop.

"*Run!*" shouted Travis.

"HEY! WHAT'RE YOU KIDS UP TO?"

It was Booker, all right. The same insulting, angry voice that used to burst out in the arena whenever a linesman missed a call.

The car door opened.

"*Wha' the hell 'r' you doin' here?*" Booker growled. He was drunk, judging by the way his words were running together.

There was no choice. They would have to run directly at the car and then break to the left, putting the vehicle between themselves and Booker.

Travis bolted first. He could hear Nish yelp behind him – the sound Nish's dog made when his tail got shut in the sliding door.

"*Hurry!*" Nish shouted.

"YOU LITTLE . . . !" Booker roared as he lunged across the hood of the Chevrolet, reaching for Nish and catching the hood of his jacket.

"NOOOOOOOO!!!!!" Nish howled. He jerked ahead with all his might, the hood tearing away slightly from his jacket, but ripping free of Booker's hand at the same time.

"*Move your butt!*" Nish screamed at Travis.

Travis was racing as fast as he could. The two Owls ran out under the brighter streetlights of Sugar Maple Drive, and turned hard to head back down towards Cedar and safety. Behind them, Travis could hear Booker's car door slamming and the engine race as the tires whined in reverse.

"*He's coming after us!*" Nish warned.

He was, too. Even in the brighter lights of Sugar Maple they could see the headlights playing in the trees as Booker reversed and turned and pulled out behind them.

The bottle! Travis knew he could run better if he wasn't cradling the empty bottle in his jacket. But he needed it for evidence.

He could hide it! And get it later . . . after they'd escaped.

Travis ran quickly to the side of the nearest snowbank and screwed the bottle down under the soft snow at the top.

Nish was now ahead of him. Travis could almost feel the headlights on his back; Booker was flicking his lights, from high beam to low, and he was gathering speed on the slippery street.

We don't want another accident! Travis thought. He was sure Booker was drunk, and he knew the alcohol would slow his reflexes. They had to deke him just as if they were playing a hockey game.

"*Next — corner!*" Travis shouted through his puffs. "*Turn — sharp — on — him!*"

With the car now roaring right behind them, they came to the next side street, and just as they seemed to be bolting straight through the intersection, both boys turned hard to the right.

Travis could hear Booker's car horn blast as the Chevrolet's weight carried it right past the turn and down the street, the brakes on full and the tires sliding helplessly.

"He'll come back!" said Nish.

"I think so, too," said Travis.

"Where next, then?" Nish asked. It was a good question. This street was another dead end.

"*Head for Mr. Dickens's!*" Travis shouted. "We'll duck in there till he goes."

Nish was already headed towards Mr. Dickens's driveway on the corner. The boys raced past the garbage and stopped at the side door, where a light burned brightly.

"What'll we tell him?" Travis asked.

"Nothing," said Nish. "He's a good guy – he won't even ask."

Nish pushed the buzzer. Pushed it again just as headlights swept down the empty street. There was a shadow at the door window, peering out.

It was Mr. Dickens. They were safe!

The door popped open.

"Whad're you boys up to?" Mr. Dickens asked. He was smiling, but seemed nervous, almost blushing.

"*There's a guy in a car chasing us!*" Nish said. Good old Nish – always right to the point.

Mr. Dickens stuck his head out the door. He was quite red in the face now. *Anger?* Travis wondered. *The cold?*

"I don't see anybody," Mr. Dickens said.

"He just went by again," said Travis.

"Can you give us a ride home?" Nish asked, again to the point.

Mr. Dickens looked stricken. *Was he afraid of Booker, too? . . . No, how could he be? He didn't know who was chasing them.*

"Can't," Mr. Dickens said, shaking his head vigorously. "No can do – car's not running right."

Travis couldn't shake the feeling that Mr. Dickens was hoping they'd just go away. *Did he not believe them?*

"Who's chasing you, anyway?" Mr. Dickens asked. He still hadn't asked them in.

"Some guy who thought we were firing snowballs at him," Nish invented.

Mr. Dickens turned and stared hard at Nish. "Were you?"

"No, sir. We didn't throw anything at anybody."

Mr. Dickens looked once more down the street. "Well," he said. "Whoever he was, he's gone now."

It was clear to Travis that they weren't going to get invited in, and he was almost glad. The warm air from inside the house smelled sickly sweet, and of smoke. Not clean and fresh like his own home, or Nish's home. And there was something not right about Mr. Dickens. He seemed to have a bad cold. Maybe that was why he'd been so reluctant to help them out.

Mr. Dickens closed the door on them, shutting off the flow of warm air and unpleasant smells.

Nish turned, his face puzzled. "What got into him?"

"I don't know."

"Maybe he's sick," said Nish.

"Maybe."

They were still standing on Mr. Dickens's porch. They scanned both directions.

"I don't see the lights any more," said Travis.

"It's all clear," said Nish. "Let's get out of here."

"We've got to go back for the bottle," Travis said.

They hurried down the driveway and back up the street until they came to the spot where Travis had hidden the bottle. It took them a minute to find it in the powdered snow. Travis held the bottle up towards the streetlight, turning it carefully.

"What's wrong?" asked Nish.

"This isn't a whisky bottle," said Travis, turning the label towards Nish. "It's rum – Captain Morgan's rum."

13

THEY HAD THE WRONG BOTTLE!

"Maybe Booker drinks rum, too," suggested Nish.

"Maybe," Travis said. But something didn't feel right.

Booker could be someone who drank a bit of everything, of course. And besides, finding a Seagram's bottle at Booker's house wouldn't really have proven anything anyway, apart from the fact that Booker and the hit-and-run driver bought the same drink. But at least it would have been a clue, one that was linked to the scene of the accident and their only other clue: the piece of metal from an unknown Chevrolet.

Nish took the bottle and twisted off the cap. He sniffed the opening quickly, and jerked his head back. "Yuck! Makes you want to throw up without even drinking!"

Nish pushed the opened bottle towards Travis, who instinctively turned away. But then Travis turned back, sniffing hard.

"Let me see that."

Nish handed over the bottle with a puzzled look, and Travis took it, sniffed again, wrinkled his nose, sniffed yet again.

"You're supposed to drink it," Nish said, "not *inhale* it."

"This isn't anything like what I smelled when Data got hit," Travis said.

"We know that. This is a rum bottle, not whisky, remember?"

"But it isn't even *close* to what whisky smells like."

"The accident was weeks ago – how can you even remember?"

"Because I just smelled it again a few minutes ago."

Nish blinked, waiting.

"At Mr. Dickens's."

It took a moment for it all to register. The eerily familiar, sweet smell of whisky coming out the front door, the red face of Mr. Dickens, his strange, unwelcoming behaviour.

Of course, thought Travis, *that's what was wrong with him. He wasn't sick. He didn't have a cold. Mr. Dickens was drunk! And maybe that's why he wouldn't drive them home; he was afraid to drive after what had happened before . . .*

"We have to go back," Travis said.

"Not again!" said Nish. "He'll be watching for us this time!"

"Not to Booker's – to Mr. Dickens's. I want to check his garbage."

This time they crept up warily on Mr. Dickens's house, crouching low. The lights were still on, but there was no movement. Travis crouched even lower and scooted across the driveway to where Mr. Dickens had put out the garbage. On the other side of the bags was the blue recycling box.

It was full of cans. Only cans. Bean cans, corn cans, chopped-fruit cans, tomato-sauce cans, spaghetti cans . . . No bottles at all!

Travis desperately searched for a telltale glint of glass. But there was nothing. It was hard to believe someone could get through so many cans in a week; they almost seemed to have been arranged there on purpose.

Too perfect, he thought. He dug deeper, removing one can after another.

Glass glinted below!

Travis reached down and pulled a bottle free. He spun the cap off and sniffed, once.

The same sickeningly sweet smell.

He spun the bottle towards the best light.

Seagram's V.O. rye whisky.

Travis now had the clue he and Nish had been looking for – even if it had shown up in an unexpected place – but he also knew that it didn't really prove anything.

Finding the right kind of whisky bottle was no better than finding the right make of car. It seemed half the people in town drove Chevrolets, and the whisky was probably the most popular brand on the market.

Mr. Dickens was also one of the best-liked people in town. He was well-known and well-respected. His garage had an excellent reputation for good work and honesty. But still, Travis couldn't shake a gut feeling. Mr. Dickens had behaved so strangely when they'd come to his door seeking safety.

The garage! Of course, Travis thought. Mr. Dickens's garage! Where no one would ever need to know what work had been done. Not if you owned the garage. Not if you did the work yourself!

Travis felt sick. Sick because suddenly he felt certain it *had* been Mr. Dickens that night. Sick because someone like Mr. Dickens had lied and then tried to hide what had happened. And sick because, while he had two real clues – the Chevrolet and the empty whisky bottle – everything else added up to pure speculation.

All Travis really had was a gut feeling. And gut feelings didn't count for anything with the police.

Travis shook his head in despair, and when he thought of what Mr. Dickens had done to Data, he wanted to cry.

14

THE NEXT DAY, THE SCREECH OWLS PRACTISED
after school. The big day of the charity game, and
the Owls' rematch against Orillia, was less than a
week away, and Muck had a lot of "little things"
he wanted them to work on.

Muck skated the Owls hard. Nish called these
skates "no-brainers," and it was as good a description as any, Travis thought. The last thing in the
world you wanted to do out there was think
about what you were doing: skating hard in both
directions, stops and starts, turning backwards on
one whistle, forward on two whistles. If you
thought about it, it seemed to hurt more. If you
thought about nothing – treated it as a no-brainer
– it seemed to go faster and, somehow, hurt less.

But this day Travis couldn't command a no-
brainer. He tried to think about what it would be
like to see all those wonderful heroes of hockey
history: Henderson, Sittler, McDonald, Shack,
Mahovlich ... He tried to think about the comedy
tricks the Flying Fathers would pull. Was it really
true they had a *horse* that could play hockey?

But nothing worked: all he could think about

was Data and what had happened since he had suggested they try "hitching."

The whistle blew loud and long: Muck's signal to pack it in and head for centre ice.

Travis and Sarah flew around the far net, sweaters rippling in the wind. Sarah let out a whoop of appreciation. The no-brainer was over!

Nish had anticipated Muck's whistle and broken away early. He'd ignored the last net they were supposed to circle and had cut fast to centre, stopping before Muck in a fine spray and immediately bowing down on his knees, breathing hard and deep, the sweat dripping from his face as if he'd just sprayed it with the Gatorade bottle.

Travis and Sarah skated up laughing. Nish hadn't fooled anyone. Muck would have seen him skating around in the rear and then cutting out early, hoping to fool the coach into thinking he, not Sarah, had been leading the hard skate.

"Okay, you've earned it," Muck said. "Black against white."

Everyone whooped this time. Sarah and Travis and Lars slammed their sticks hard against the ice. *Black against white.* They were going to scrimmage.

Practice was never better than when they finished up with a good scrimmage. Scrimmage was the best kind of hockey, Travis thought. They could try out the plays they'd been daydreaming about. There weren't even any parents in the stands to watch. That was one good effect of the no-brainer: the parents had all gone off in search of fresh coffee or newspapers. Anything to avoid watching.

"Black against white" meant dark sweaters against light – Sarah's line against Andy's, Lars's defence against Nish's, the other players all divided up evenly.

Muck tossed the puck to Ty, his assistant, and carefully pulled the whistle off over his head and placed it on the bench in the penalty box. He then adjusted the small shin pads he wore, punched his gloves tight and skated back to defence, where he tapped Nish on the pads.

Nish understood immediately. Even if it was only a scrimmage, he shouldn't play with his broken wrist. Nish shook his head, pretending to be outraged, and skated off happily.

Ty reached out and let the puck fall, and Travis felt a chill run up his spine. Nothing to do with the cold. Nothing to do with how much he'd been sweating. *Everything* to do with seeing Muck there, his stick ready, back arched, just the way Data would wait.

Sarah plucked the puck out of the air and cuffed a quick backhand over to Travis, who circled back, lifting his head to see if he had a play. Sarah was pounding her stick as she jumped through centre, racing towards the other blueline.

Travis sent a saucer pass over Jesse's stick that was perfectly timed. But for *Muck*, not Sarah!

Laughing, Muck knocked the puck out of the air with the blade of his stick. He moved quickly, as fast as his bad leg would allow, up across centre, where Lars was racing back to check him.

Muck simply shifted his big body to block Lars from the puck. Then, still laughing, he came in along the far side of the boards. Jenny moved out from the net in anticipation – her catching glove snapping like a lobster claw, her pads wiggling as she moved forward.

Muck wound up for a slapshot. Jenny readied herself. Muck looked up, then ripped a hard pass across the ice to where Jesse Highboy, flying in from the blueline, merely had to tip the puck into an empty net.

Muck and the "whites" high-fived and screamed in the corner. Muck came skating out, slammed his stick on the ice and teased Travis.

"Thanks for the pass."

Travis smiled sheepishly. He'd been so proud of his little saucer pass to Sarah. It had led to a perfect goal – but by Muck and the "whites," not Travis's "black" team.

They played for almost twenty minutes. Travis wondered why Muck was letting them play so long. But then, as time went on, he came to realize the scrimmage wasn't just for them.

Muck was having as much fun as anyone.

15

"TRAVIS, YOU'VE GOTTA COME AND SEE WHAT we're doing," Fahd said the next day as school was getting out.

"I'm supposed to go over to my grandparents'," Travis said. "My dad's picking me up there."

"It'll just take a minute," said Fahd.

"Okay, but make it fast."

Fahd led Travis down to Mrs. Wheeler's room, where they were deep in preparations for the mock disaster that would take place the week after Data's big night.

The windows of Mrs. Wheeler's room were covered up with paper to prevent the rest of the school from standing around gawking. Inside, they were preparing "bodies" for the practice disaster. They were making crash victims and burn victims and even what Fahd called "a bloody axe murder," though to Travis it looked more like a store dummy that had been cut up by a chainsaw and coated with spaghetti sauce.

"Gruesome, eh?" said Fahd. "*I love it.*"

Some of it was gruesome, some of it was stupid, thought Travis. But when he saw some dummies being prepared to stage an automobile crash, he shuddered. These ones were spooky.

Fahd opened the door that led into the art room.

"This," said Fahd, "is where we work on *real* bodies."

Inside, there were student volunteers in white coats and other students lying on tables.

"We have to have 'real' victims, too," said Fahd. "I'm being trained in disaster make-up. These are living survivors we'll be taking to the emergency ward by ambulance. The doctors and nurses have to treat them like they are really hurt. The kids even have to answer questions about their injuries – except, of course, for those who'll come in 'unconscious.'"

Travis stared around the room, open-mouthed. He recognized some of the students on the tables, but now they looked exactly like crash victims and burn victims, bloodied and bandaged, some with their skulls shattered, eyes destroyed, arms and legs broken. Only instead of screaming in pain, they were talking – even laughing.

"Neat, eh?" said Fahd.

"Yeah," said Travis, "neat. But I gotta get going."

"Okay," said Fahd. "Hope you don't have trouble getting to sleep tonight."

Travis didn't need to wait until bedtime to have a nightmare. All the way to his grandparents' place he thought of nothing but car accidents and broken bodies and what on earth he was going to do about finding the person who had hit Data.

But *what* could he do? He was going over the clues and what, if anything, he could tell the police. He needed proof – not guesswork. But by the time he reached his grandparents' house, he was still only guessing.

Travis's grandmother was a character. She had a great, huge laugh and was about as far removed from anyone's idea of an old woman as Travis could imagine. She worked out almost every day. She wore a tracksuit more often than a dress. She listened to the "Golden Oldies" radio station, usually singing along. And she was never so happy as when she was at the cottage, curled up in her hammock beneath the pines, sipping a cold beer straight from the bottle while reading a mystery novel.

Of course, Travis thought, mystery novels. If anyone would know how to help him, his grandmother Lindsay would. The bookcases at their house were full of mysteries. And every week she watched British mysteries on Public Television. Her favourite character was Miss Marple, a crime solver who looked exactly the way Travis thought a grandmother was supposed to look. You'd never catch Miss Marple drinking beer straight from the bottle.

Travis's grandmother put out some oatmeal cookies and made Travis some hot chocolate and, before he knew it, Travis was telling her everything he knew about what had happened since the night of the accident.

"So you know who did it," she said when Travis was finished, "but there's no proof."

"We *think* we know," said Travis. "But that's not enough. The police would just laugh at us."

"You should read more mystery novels," Travis's grandmother smiled. "The police are *always* the last to clue in."

"But we're just kids," said Travis. "No one listens to us, anyway."

"*I'm* listening, young man."

His grandmother sat for a while, staring at Travis as he munched on his cookie.

"A guilty party," she said finally, more to herself than to Travis, "but no clue strong enough to stand up." She had one finger pressed tight to her lips, thinking.

Suddenly she stood up, a look of determination on her face, and walked towards the doorway.

"Where are you going?" Travis asked.

"I'll be right back," she said over her shoulder.

Travis could hear her poking around in her bookcases.

"*Aha!*" he heard her exclaim.

She came back into the kitchen, thumping the book on her hand. "I knew Miss Marple would have been through that," she said, setting the book down so Travis could read the cover. It was *The Moving Finger*, by Agatha Christie.

"This is about a drunk driver?" Travis asked.

"No," his grandmother smiled. "But it *is* about catching a murderer when there is absolutely no evidence and the criminal is considered one of the most upstanding citizens in town."

Travis grabbed at the book, turning the pages, fast. "How do they catch him?" he asked.

"Miss Marple," said his grandmother, "sets a brilliant trap."

Travis finished the book in three nights, reading until his mother called for him to turn out his lights. He was fascinated, and frightened.

Miss Marple had indeed encountered a similar situation. A body turns up, and no one – no one but Miss Marple – suspects foul play. There is no evidence. There is only her own suspicion that one of the village's best-known and most-respected citizens is hiding something. She sets an ingenious trap, and it works perfectly.

There was a passage in the final chapter of *The Moving Finger* that Travis read twice. A man is criticizing Miss Marple for having put them all in danger:

"My dear young man," Miss Marple had answered. "*Something* had to be done. There was no evidence against this very clever and unscrupulous man. I needed someone to help me, someone of high courage and good brains. I found the person I needed."

"It was very dangerous for her."

"Yes, it was dangerous, but we are not put into this world . . . to avoid danger when an innocent person's life is at stake. You understand me?"

Travis understood. Now he needed "someone of high courage and good brains."

And he knew just the person to turn to.

16

"NO WAY!"

Travis had expected this response from Nish. He knew his plan was the stuff of books, not real life, but they had no choice.

"Maybe we can get him to confess," argued Travis. "It works in books."

"Books are stupid," said Nish.

"You're stupid," replied Travis. He couldn't help thinking that maybe he should have gone somewhere else to find "someone of high courage and good brains."

"Tell me how it could possibly work, then," Nish said, "if you're so smart."

Travis half made the plan up as he went along, hoping that once it was all said, it might somehow make sense.

If the trap was going to have any chance, Dickens would have to be in his car and he would have to be drunk again.

But Nish's questions were only beginning. How would they know Mr. Dickens was drunk again and driving?

Well, they'd have to be lucky on that part, Travis admitted, but he felt there was a good chance.

How would they get him to stop?

Well, they'd have to trick him. Maybe get him to think he'd hit someone again.

How would he *think* he'd hit someone?

"Well . . . Fahd," said Travis.

"*What?*" said Nish.

"Fahd," Travis repeated. He'd had an idea. A sudden, flashing idea. Perhaps even a brilliant one. "Fahd can help us."

"*Absolutely no way!*" Nish shouted this time.

But no one was listening to Nish. The others – Fahd, Sarah, Andy, and Lars – had embraced Travis's idea immediately. Sarah came up with the idea of setting the trap along Cedar and River, exactly where the original accident had happened. Andy thought of the snowball. Lars was already trying to calculate the timing and wanted to do a few dry runs first. Fahd thought about how to set things up for the best effect.

Travis kept his doubts to himself. If he was wrong, if Mr. Dickens hadn't done it, it was going to be a huge waste of time. But they had to try.

Nish, on the other hand, had no problem expressing his doubts.

"*No way!*" he repeated.

"Oh, come on, Nish," said Sarah. "Only you can pull it off. You're the best moaner I ever heard."

Travis knew that Nish would never really turn down the starring role. Everything, in the end, would depend on him.

Nish closed his eyes tight, opened them, blinked, and chewed his lip. Finally he spoke.

"Okay, let's do it."

It took three evenings before the conditions were right for the Owls' daring plan.

Mr. Dickens's car had been found parked behind the bar down by River Street. It had snowed hard earlier in the day, and some of the streets had still not been ploughed. Most of the cars were snow-covered, and, just like the last time, some were being driven with "portholes" dug through the snow on the windshield, with no view at all through the rear window.

Lars had a large flashlight in his coat pocket. He and Sarah would stand watch and be able to signal from the far corner when Dickens turned onto Cedar on his way home. Andy and Travis were responsible for making the huge snowballs. Lars had timed a couple of trial runs, and now one was packed and ready at the top of the hill at the edge of the schoolyard. If they pushed off just as a car passed by the church, it would smack right into its side as it passed below the hill.

Fahd's job was toughest of all. He had to make Nish look like he'd just been hit by a car.

Fahd's mock-disaster training was key. He had become an expert on gory, slimy, bloody entrails and broken bones and missing eyes and caved-in skulls. For nearly a month, every day had been like Hallowe'en to Fahd. But his big test wouldn't be the mock disaster. It would be tonight.

"*He's ready!*" Fahd called up the hill.

Travis and Andy watched as Fahd attended to Nish, whose leg seemed set at a weird angle. It was bent all wrong, and he seemed to be shuffling along on his other leg. But then they realized: Nish had put both feet through one pant leg, the other, shattered one was phony.

They could barely make Nish out in the street-light. But then, he hardly had a face any more. He had one eye knocked clear of its socket. It was hanging down his face, suspended by stringy flesh and bouncing off his cheek. He had a huge, black wound on his forehead. His mouth was bleeding, the teeth hanging out one side through a hole where his cheek should have been.

"You look awful!" Travis shouted down.

"I do?" Nish answered, pretending to be surprised. "Funny, I feel *great*."

"Hurry up!" snapped Fahd. "We can't have him see us."

"*The light!*" Andy shouted. Lars was flashing the signal.

"*Hurry!*" Fahd hissed. He grabbed Nish's "broken" leg and pulled him along by it, forcing Nish to hop to stay upright. They ducked into the nearest driveway, their heads down.

Travis and Andy got behind the giant snowball. They were well out of sight, and could look around to see what was coming.

A snow-covered car was weaving down Cedar. Only half the windshield had been cleaned, and the car was drifting from side to side. From behind, the flashlight signalled again – confirmation from Lars that it was Mr. Dickens, for sure.

"I hope this works," said Andy as he leaned against the huge snowball.

"*It has to!*" said Travis.

Travis watched, his heart pounding. The car passed by the last of the houses, the church manse, the church itself, the church drive . . .

"*Now!*"

The two boys heaved with all their might. The huge snowball groaned, and began to move.

"*Push!*" Travis called. Andy grunted loudly, and the ball rolled. It was off, gaining speed.

Travis's heart skipped a beat. The car fishtailed slightly, then straightened. The snowball rolled down and up slightly at the bank, then flew out into the air.

He has to see it! Travis said to himself.

It's going to miss! was his next thought.

But Travis's imagination was also airborne, moving faster than the giant snowball. It seemed as if the ball was hanging in midair. It seemed as if the car was stopped. The ball hanging, the car frozen – and nothing but his own hammering heart to mark the passage of time.

"*Perfect!*" Andy whispered.

And it was, too. With an enormous *whomp!* the snowball hit squarely against the passenger door.

The car lurched violently to the side. Whether it was the force of the snowball or Mr. Dickens's frightened reaction, Travis couldn't tell, but the big Chevrolet swung against the far bank and came to a stop in deep snow.

"*C'mon, Nish! Move it!*"

The voice was Fahd's. Travis could hear the fear it contained; Fahd was nearly hysterical.

From the near driveway, two small figures hurried out, the one in front straining ahead, the one behind hopping madly.

"*Hold your horses!*" Nish hissed. "*I don't want my make-up to run!*"

Travis couldn't help himself. He started to giggle. He felt Andy grab his elbow, pulling him down out of sight.

Travis could see Fahd, the perfectionist, laying Nish out in exactly the position he wanted. It seemed almost comic – if it weren't so dangerous! He wondered if they'd make it in time.

A door opened on the Chevrolet. Greenish light spilled out onto the street. It was the passenger door, as the driver's door was now hard against the far bank. A large figure was struggling to get out of the car. He was wearing a dark coat. And a tuque.

Travis shivered. He had seen that same figure before, and in this very spot.

"*Damn it all t' hell!*" a voice was cursing.

Fahd was already away, scrambling back up the near driveway. Travis looked up the street. He thought he saw two small figures crouching down as they hurried along. It would be Sarah and Lars.

Now it was all up to Nish.

Travis shut his eyes: *For Data, Nish, for Data . . .*

The moaning began soft and low.

"Ohhhhhhhhhhhhhhhhhhhhhhhhhhhh . . .

"OHHHHHHH . . . Owwwwww.

"*H-h-h-help me! Help . . . mmeee!*

"OWWWWWWWW!"

The figure was out of the car now and standing on the hard-packed snow of the street.

"*Wha' the hell!*" he muttered.

He took a couple of steps forward, slipped and went down on one knee. He cursed angrily.

Nish moaned again, softly: "Ohhhhhhhhh . . . Ohhhhhhhhhhhh . . ."

The man regained his footing and stepped forward, uneasily.

"*H-h-h-help me! Help . . . mmeee!*" wailed Nish.

"*Oh, goodness, no . . . no . . . no!*" the man said. He came closer, close enough to see the twisted leg, close enough, perhaps, to see the smashed head of poor Nish, dying in the street.

"*Oh, Lord, no – this can't be happening! Why me?*"

Why me? Travis thought. This man is standing there feeling sorry for *himself* while he's already put one kid in hospital and another is bleeding to death in front of his very eyes.

The man came even closer, close enough to lean down and touch Nish, if he wanted.

Nish was silent. *Dead* silent!

The driver seemed to stand, staring, for the longest time. He didn't reach out for Nish. He didn't lean down.

Good! thought Travis. If he gets too close, he might see it's a trick. And if he finds out it's a trick, Nish might just as well be dead.

The man seemed to lean forward a little, perhaps about to bend down and help, but then he stepped back, stumbled, and appeared to stare in new horror at poor Nish, lying broken and bloody in the snow.

Nish picked his moment well: "*H-h-h-help me! Help . . . mmeee!*"

But the man couldn't do it. The urge to save himself was stronger than the urge to help. He turned, slipping again to one knee, and with another curse got up and bolted for his car.

"*What do we do now?*" hissed Andy.

"*I don't know.*"

The man slipped and slid and cursed his way to the passenger door of the Chevrolet, ripped the door open, and jumped back in. The engine was still running.

He put the car in gear and slammed down on the gas. The car bucked, then sank into the snowbank some more.

He put it in reverse and hit the gas again. The car jumped but only settled in deeper.

He rammed the transmission from reverse to forward, to reverse again, back and forth, the car bucking like a horse but unable to spring free of the deep snow.

The door flew open again, and the man spilled out, swearing. "*Damn it all to hell! . . . Damn it . . . damn it . . . damn it! Why me?*"

"*Drunk as a skunk!*" Andy said, almost under his breath.

The man had no intention of going back to help Nish. He slammed the door and began to stumble down the street, slipping and sliding, lurching his way home, trying to run away from what he had done – for the second time.

"*He's getting away!*" Fahd cried as he came out from behind his snowbank.

Nish was sitting up, watching him go.

"It doesn't matter," Travis said as he and Andy scrambled down towards them.

"Whatdya mean it doesn't matter?" Nish asked, trying to yank off his "broken" leg. "The guy who did this to me should go to jail!"

"It doesn't matter," said Travis, "because we have his car."

17

"I SEE," SAID MR. LINDSAY INTO THE TELEPHONE. "Thank you very much, then . . . Yes, I will . . . Goodbye."

Travis's father hung up the phone. He took a sip from his coffee and stared out the window towards the bird feeder, which was alive with chickadees fighting over sunflower seeds.

"*Well?*" Mrs. Lindsay said, waiting.

Mr. Lindsay turned quickly, almost as if he were snapping back into reality.

"That was the police," he said slowly. "There's been a development in the hit-and-run incident."

"What?"

It seemed Mr. Lindsay didn't even want to say at first. He shook his head. "It was Tony Dickens."

"Tony *Dickens* was the one who hit Data?"

"Apparently. Funny, I always thought he was a first-class person."

"Would you like a list of the 'respectable' people who have been caught drinking and driving?" said Mrs. Lindsay. "Let alone a list of those who *haven't* been caught?"

"I know, I know. It's just that he was always so good with kids. I backed him for the presidency of the hockey association one year, you know."

"You can never tell what people are really like," Mrs. Lindsay said. "How did they catch him, anyway?"

"The police found his car ditched along Cedar. Called in at his house and he was sitting in his kitchen, crying. Confessed it all right there and then, without their even saying a word to him."

"A guilty conscience, I guess."

"Guilty's hardly the word for it," said Mr. Lindsay. "Kept claiming he'd hit *two* kids, not one."

Mrs. Lindsay went back to her magazine. "Well, hard drink will do that to you, won't it?"

Mr. Lindsay was again looking out the window. The chickadees fluttered wildly as a squirrel dropped down onto the feeder.

"I guess."

Travis Lindsay, sitting quietly over a bowl of Cheerios, could barely conceal his smile as he bit into another spoonful.

18

TRAVIS HAD NEVER FELT SUCH ELECTRICITY IN the Tamarack Arena. There must have been two thousand fans jammed into the stands this Sunday afternoon, and the cheering had started the moment the first of the Maple Leafs Legends had stepped out onto the ice.

"*Lanny McDonald!*" Fahd had called.

It was indeed – hair a bit thinner than in his picture on the hockey card, but his moustache still red and thick as a broom.

"*Frank Mahovlich!*" Jesse shouted.

And after Mahovlich, Darryl Sittler . . . Eddie Shack . . . Paul Henderson . . .

"Where's Muck?" Travis asked, straining to see.

"There," said Sarah, pointing.

But Muck didn't look like Muck. He was wearing full equipment, and a beautiful Maple Leafs Legends sweater. Travis noticed the number first – 6, same as Data – and then the name sewn over the number: Munro.

Out on the ice surface, Muck looked smaller

than some of the other players, but his passes were the same as the rest of the Legends': crisp, hard, and perfectly tape to tape.

The Flying Fathers were hilarious. Perhaps this was *called* a hockey game, but it didn't always seem like one. When Lanny McDonald scored the first goal of the game, the Flying Fathers held a ceremony at centre ice where they made Lanny kneel, and then "blessed" him with a cream pie straight in the face.

The crowd loved it. The best of the Flying Fathers, perhaps the best skater on the ice, pulled a trick that had Travis laughing so hard his stomach hurt. At the face-off the referee only faked dropping the puck, and instead the Father dropped his own puck, which he'd hidden in his glove. It looked exactly like a normal face-off, except that this puck was attached by fishing line to the player's stick.

He took off up the ice, stickhandling so wildly it seemed the puck would shoot off into the stands. But each time it came back, perfectly, to the blade of his stick. He went around every laughing, staggering NHLer, Muck included, and then tossed his stick – puck included – into the NHL net. The red light came on. Tie game.

The Legends protested, but it was useless. The Fathers played with illegal sticks and even brought out illegal players – including, at one point, their horse! With one of the Fathers holding onto its tail, it galloped down the ice, clearing the track, and the Father simply threw the puck into the net.

In the final period, however, they all settled down to a real game of hockey.

Perhaps it was a little slower than an NHL game, but the skill shone through: the passes, the quick, hard, accurate shots, the fine little plays that would instantly leave a man open, with only the goal-tender between him and the net.

Halfway through the third, the Owls started up a chant.

"*Muck . . . Muck . . . Muck . . . MUCK!*"

Soon much of the crowd had joined in.

"*Muck . . . Muck . . . Muck . . . MUCK!*"

There was no doubt the Screech Owls' coach heard, but no way was he going to show he had heard. He was on Paul Henderson's line, just as they had been as teenagers so many years before, and while Henderson could still fly down the ice, it was apparent to all who were watching that Muck's bad leg was holding him back.

When Henderson's line was off for a shift, Mr. Dillinger made his way over to Muck and unlaced the coach's skate and removed his pads. Mr. Dillinger had an aerosol can in his hand.

All the Owls could see what was happening. They'd seen it before in NHL games. Mr. Dillinger aimed the can and sprayed up and down Muck's bad leg, "freezing" it to reduce the pain. Muck was gritting his teeth and holding his bare leg out so Mr. Dillinger could cover it entirely.

Two shifts later, Henderson's line came back out, with Muck testing his leg cautiously on the ice. Travis could see that Muck was in real pain.

Partway through the shift, Paul Henderson darted back after a loose puck. No sooner had he picked it up than Muck was rapping his stick hard on the ice on the far side. Henderson passed hard and right on target, the puck cracking solidly onto Muck's blade and sticking.

Muck dug in, his gait slightly off as he gathered speed. He neatly stepped around the first checker and then shifted into centre ice and bore down. He was over the Fathers' line, with two defencemen back, both backpedalling and tightening the knot on Muck.

Muck slipped the puck ahead and jumped – *jumped* – clean through the gap between the two defenders, both of whom were laughing as they crashed together, nothing between them but air.

Muck wobbled slightly as he landed, but kept his footing. He still had the puck.

He wound up and snapped a shot, high and hard.

The goalie's glove hand whipped out, but like the defenders found nothing but air.

The puck rang off the crossbar – *and in!*

As the red light flashed on, the arena seemed to explode.

"ALLL RIGHHHHT, MUCK!" Sarah screamed, leaping to her feet.

It turned out to be the winning goal, as if anyone really cared. The crowd was already on its feet, screaming and cheering as the final seconds wound down and the horn sounded. Even before the referee blew his final whistle, the Flying Fathers and the Maple Leafs Legends were shaking hands and hugging each other.

Travis watched Muck. The Owls' coach was grinning from ear to ear. They were slapping him on the back.

Muck seemed concerned about something else, though. He was looking for Paul Henderson. And when he found him talking to the Flying Fathers' goaltender, Muck skated over and held his own stick out towards his old friend.

Paul Henderson laughed and happily exchanged sticks with Muck.

So, Travis thought to himself, there was a little bit of the kid in Muck Munro. He was after a souvenir.

"Let's go," Sarah said, yanking on Travis's jacket sleeve.

Travis turned, about to ask, "Where?"

"We're on next," Sarah said. "We should already be dressed."

"I CAN GO."

The Screech Owls had dressed without Muck, who was still changing with the Legends. The dressing room was silent but for the determined voice of Wayne Nishikawa, injured defenceman.

"*I can go,*" he repeated.

No one else spoke. Mr. Dillinger had gone off to fill his water bottles.

Travis figured, as captain, it was his duty to take control of the situation.

"You can't," Travis said gently. "Your wrist."

But Nish was already almost dressed.

"I've got my new cast," he said.

"What if you get hit?" Sarah asked. There was genuine concern in her voice.

Nish looked up, smiled. "I've got a secret weapon."

No one asked what.

Nish dug into a side pocket of his equipment bag and pulled out a spray can – the same can Mr. Dillinger had sprayed on Muck's bad leg.

Freezing.

"You *can't*!" Sarah said.

"Mind your own business," Nish said. "I've already sprayed my arm once. I'll do it again between periods."

"Where'd you get that?" Travis asked.

"It was on the Legends' bench at the end of the game. Nobody was around, so I . . . borrowed it. I'll put it back after our game."

"You shouldn't," Sarah warned.

"Maybe not," Nish smiled. "But I already did – so let's get out there."

Travis knew there was no use arguing.

Travis led the Owls out onto the fresh ice surface, stunned, as he stepped onto the ice, to realize that the huge crowd that had turned out for the big game had stayed! For an ordinary peewee regular-season game!

He checked the crowd as he waited for his turn to shoot. He could see his parents and grandparents. His grandmother gave him the thumbs-up. He wondered if she had guessed about the trap they had set for Mr. Dickens.

He scanned the seats on the other side and saw that a section had been set aside for some older men, some of them vaguely familiar. And then he realized:

That moustache could only belong to Lanny McDonald!

And there was Paul Henderson! And the rest of the Maple Leafs Legends! And the Flying Fathers!

They had all stayed to see the Owls play!

The puck came out to Travis and he kicked it easily up onto his stick blade. Suddenly, there was no noise, just the flick of his skates. He saw Jenny come out, her catching glove yapping at him, her pads skittering as she moved.

He deked once, moved to the outside, and shot high and hard.

Crossbar!

Travis turned and looked up into the crowd. Lanny McDonald pumped a fist at him. *He knew!* Lanny knew! An NHLer knew that there was nothing so sweet as the sound of a puck on the crossbar – so long as it wasn't in a game!

The public-address system crackled. There would be a ceremonial face-off. Travis wondered who it would be to drop the puck. Maybe Paul Henderson himself. That was probably why all the hockey heroes had stayed. He stood by Sarah, waiting for a name.

But there was none. The public-address system was silent.

Then all around him the crowd began to rise. All through the arena there was the sound of people getting to their feet. And with it came the sound of applause. A few began clapping at first, and then dozens, then hundreds – the sound growing as loud as thunder.

Travis followed the direction of the crowd's stares.

The Zamboni entrance was open. Muck was there, and Muck's big hands were on a wheelchair.

And in the chair was Data!

The clapping became a roar as the crowd realized what was going on.

Muck pushed out and the chair rolled onto the ice. Data slowly raised the one arm he could move. He had his Screech Owls jacket on. He was smiling.

Travis turned to look at his teammates. Sarah was bawling, her glove uselessly wiping at the huge tears dropping off her cheek.

Muck rolled Data along the blueline, passing by each Owl, and Data reached out to tap the gloves of each player. Muck stopped, and stared hard at Nish before moving ahead down the line, shaking his head.

When they got to Travis, Data held his hand up for Muck to stop again.

Data looked up and smiled a bit crookedly. "I know what you did," he said. "Thanks."

Travis tried to speak, but he couldn't. What could he say? It was his fault, after all, wasn't it? It was his idea to go "hitching." If he'd never done that, Data would be standing on the blueline instead of sitting in a wheelchair.

Muck pushed Data ahead, but not before taking one quick look at his captain. Muck's eyes seemed to be begging an explanation. But he would never get one.

Sarah and the Orillia captain took the ceremonial face-off. Sarah picked up the puck and presented it to Data with a kiss on the cheek and a long hug. Travis could see that she was still crying. And she didn't seem to care who knew.

20

IF THE OWLS HAD EVER PLAYED A GREATER GAME, Travis couldn't remember when. Every player seemed at the top of his or her game.

Data had been given a special place between Muck and Mr. Dillinger behind the bench and he cheered as loudly as he could. Muck never said a word. Not to Nish about his arm. Not to Travis about what Data had said. But Travis wondered how much Muck knew.

Sarah sent Dmitri in on a breakaway halfway through the first period for the first goal, then scored herself on a beautiful backhand deke. Travis got the third, and Wilson the fourth.

Late in the final period, with the Owls up 4–1, Travis noticed Nish wincing.

"You okay?"

"I'm fine."

But Travis knew the freezing was wearing off. Nish could barely hold his stick, but he wouldn't quit.

Sarah won the face-off and dropped the puck to Wilson, who spun back and bounced a pass off the backboards onto Nish's stick.

Nish started to rush. He moved out slowly at first, then jumped across the blueline, picking up speed.

Sarah was straight up centre, expecting the pass. But Nish held on. He carried in over the Orillia blueline and circled. He faked a pass to Travis, stepped into the slot, drew back his stick, and pounded the puck as hard as he could.

It almost went through the back of the net! Travis, circling at the side of the net, watched the twine spring and then shoot the puck back out as fast as it had come in.

The whistle blew; the referee was signalling a goal.

Nish was already halfway to the bench, crouching over to cradle his arm.

"Get – me – the – puck," he said to Travis, grunting with the effort.

Travis skated to the linesman, who was coming back with the puck. "Don't blame him," the linesman said as he handed it over. "Hardest shot I ever saw in peewee."

Travis skated back to the bench. He held the puck out towards Nish, who was bent double, holding his arm. Nish looked up, shook his head.

"For – Data," he said. "Give – it – to – him."

Travis skated further down the bench and handed it to Data. Data took the puck in his good hand as if it were an Olympic gold medal.

Muck shook his head. "Nishikawa can play this game when he wants to," he said.

"Too bad we can't freeze his brain, too," Sarah said under her breath.

The Screech Owls had won their re-match. When the final horn blew, the Orillia team lined up and shook hands, and then, in a move Travis had to admire, they skated to the Screech Owls' bench, where they took turns tapping their gloves against Data's outstretched hand.

As Travis watched he realized Data was still holding on to Nish's puck. He had never let go.

There was still one small matter of unfinished business. Before the Zamboni came out, the doors nearest the stands opened and all the Maple Leafs Legends and Flying Fathers came down onto the ice to an enormous cheer from the crowd.

Paul Henderson and Frank Mahovlich were carrying a huge rectangle of cardboard, but none of the peewee players on the ice could see what was on it. Muck and Mr. Dillinger were wheeling Data out of the home bench and onto the ice, where the photographers were waiting.

Mr. Dillinger pushed Data up to centre ice, where, with a grand flourish, Paul Henderson and Frank Mahovlich turned the big cardboard rectangle around for everyone to see.

It was a giant cheque, made out to something called The Larry Ulmar Foundation.

The amount was for thirty thousand dollars. Again the crowd roared its approval.

Travis looked back towards the bench and saw that Muck was leaning over and pulling a stick free. It was the one he'd traded with Paul Henderson.

Muck walked cautiously back over the ice, clearly trying not to limp too badly. He went over to Data and laid the stick across his lap. Data looked down at it, carefully turning the stick over and over with his one good hand.

It had been signed by all the Maple Leafs Legends and the Flying Fathers!

So that was it, Travis thought. Muck didn't want a souvenir for himself. He wanted something special for Data, something other than money that would remind him of his special day.

Travis wondered if Muck had signed it too. He hoped so. Muck had belonged with the Legends – this day, anyway.

Data took the stick and waved it at the crowd. Everyone cheered.

With Muck's help, Data turned the stick over so he could hold the blade, and he then – very slowly, with some difficulty – lifted the stick so the handle was pointing directly at his team.

It was Data's salute to the Screech Owls, *his* team forever.

THE END

THE NEXT BOOK IN THE SCREECH OWLS SERIES

Nightmare in Nagano

The Screech Owls can't believe their good luck! They are flying to Nagano, Japan, the host city for the 1998 Winter Olympic Games. It was here that, for the first time ever, stars of the NHL competed for Olympic medals and women's Olympic hockey was played.

No one is more excited than Nish, who will at last get to visit his ancestral homeland. Nish is an expert on Japan. It is a land — he tells the Owls — of electrically heated toilet seats and vending machines that sell beer!

The attractions of Japan are quickly forgotten, however, when Nish stumbles upon an ancient secret that appears to give him almost super-human powers. Mysterious forces seek to prevent Nish's discovery from becoming known, and soon his new-found knowledge has placed the lives of all the Screech Owls in danger.

Nightmare in Nagano, *the ninth book in the Screech Owls Series, will be published by McClelland & Stewart in the fall of 1998.*